DEXTRA

The blue grassy shore thronged with inhabitants of several species. There were Wildings wearing the badge of the Wheel, and green fauns, and also the strange, stocky Gobblers . . .

Also among the welcomers were a couple of human-centaurs, dressed in purple cloaks but nothing else. Finally, there was one person who stood taller than any faun Cleito had seen. His skin was bright gold and his hair green, and he wore a gorgeous gold-and-purple cloak and a diadem of blue laurel.

"We call them Silvans—or sometimes just Gods," said Will. "They are a sort of faun royalty . . . It is a tradition among us—a prophecy if you like—that one day Evenor will be their kingdom when we Wildings have moved on elsewhere. . . ."

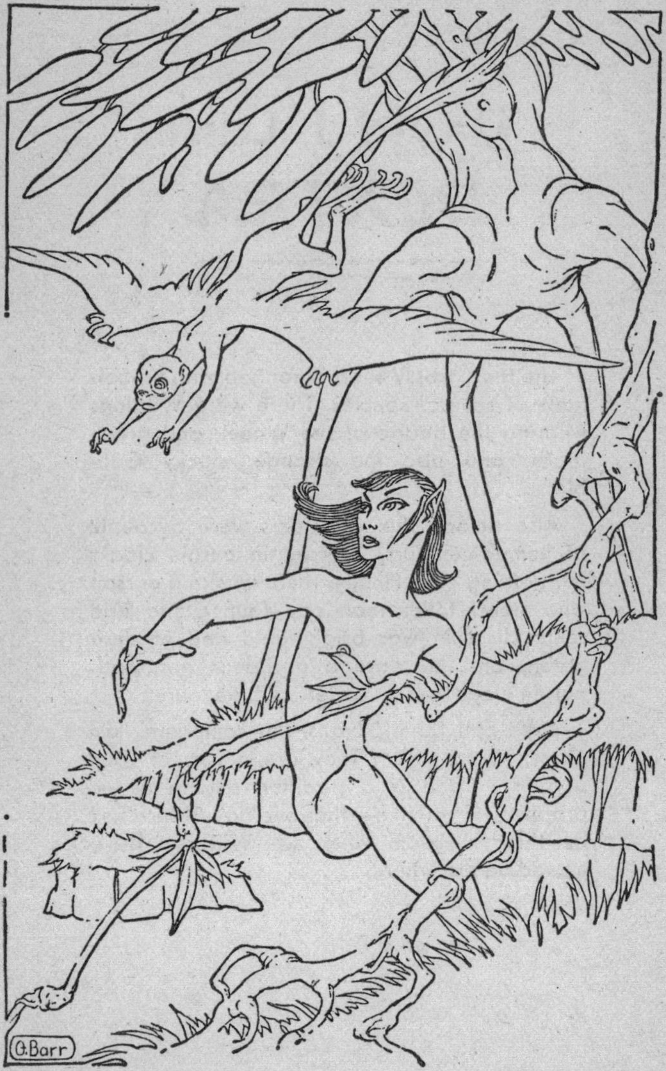
O.Barr

David J. Lake

THE
WILDINGS
OF
WESTRON

DAW BOOKS, INC.
DONALD A. WOLLHEIM, PUBLISHER

1301 Avenue of the Americas
New York, N. Y.　　10019

Copyright ©, 1977, by David J. Lake

All Rights Reserved.

Cover art by George Barr.

First printing, June 1977

1 2 3 4 5 6 7 8 9

DAW BOOKS

PRINTED IN U.S.A.

Ophelia: Lord, we know what we are, but know not what we may be . . .

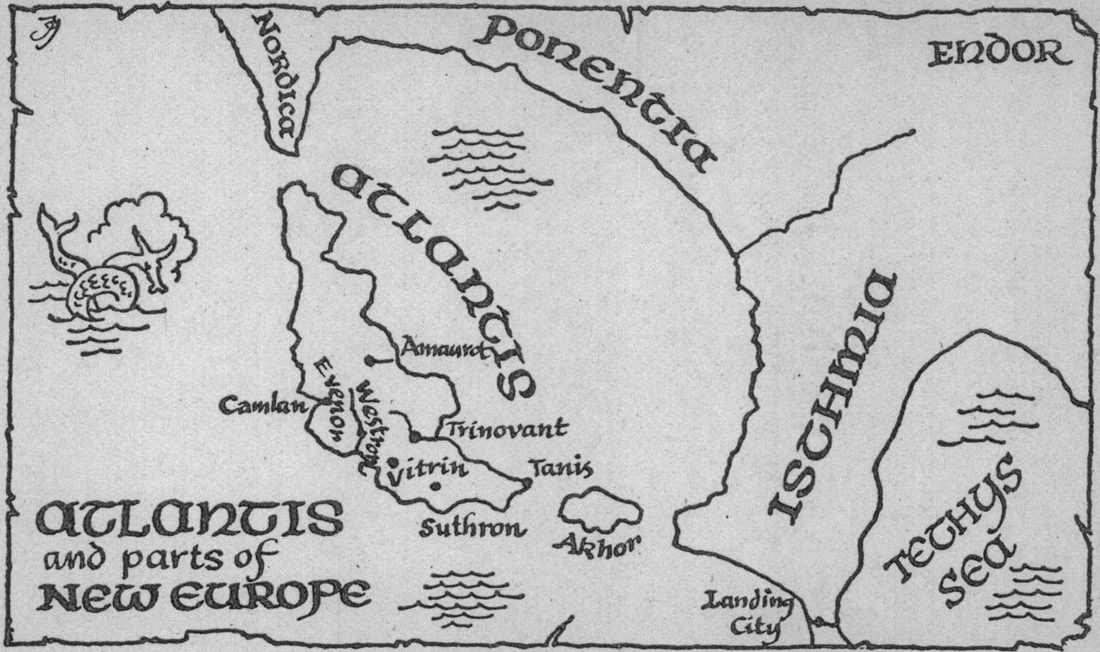
ATLANTIS
and parts of
NEW EUROPE
Endor
Ponentia
Nordica
Atlantis
Amaurot
Evenor
Westron
Camlan
Trinovant
Vitrin
Tanis
Suthron
Akhor
Isthmia
Tethys
Sea
Landing
City

PART I:

Free County

Chapter
ONE

Holy Ring, thought Cleito Dixon suddenly: I do believe the Count is looking at *me!*

She had come out, that Monday sabbat, with the rest of her family and a great many other people from the Cathedral Covenstead into the city square of Westron. It was a fine spring morning, warm for April in Atlantis, and the golden haze of the eternal clouds brought out the vivid colors everywhere. Of the burghers' doublets and the ladies' robes—mostly red, white or green, the politically safe hues; of the massive neo-Norman arches fronting the round coven-church—yellow of native sandstone; of the splendid cloaks of the Count and his retinue—blood red and gold, and sumptuous steel-gray.

But Cleito had no eyes now for pretty colors.

She was sixteen years old (seventeen by Old Reckoning), and had frequently come with her uncle's family from their farm into Westron, but she had never before seen Count Horold Harkness. This was not surprising: the Count normally kept aloof from his subjects, and of a Monday he worshipped in a different manner in his palace chapel, since he honored the sect of the Sword, not (like his people) that of the Ring. But now here he was, reining in his hexip in the great square before the Ring Cathedral—and, Cleito feared, looking straight at *her.*

The Count was at least forty years old, dark-eyed, grizzled, but still handsome, and not at all bent by the remorseless gravity of the planet Dextra. His court poets sang that there was no more gallant gentleman in the whole island of Atlantis, nay, not in all the Western World from Nordica to Livya. (The wiser poets threw in Hyperborea and Kataya as well.) They celebrated his many victories in formal battles-of-a-hundred-knights against the Counts of Vitrin and Suthron and Amaurot, and his more significant but less formal victory in the rebellion against his elder brother the Governor of Trinovant. They celebrated, too, his other sort of victories over the hearts of Court ladies—and at times (when he deigned so far) over those of humble subject-women. Cleito remembered one song a wandering minstrel had sung at their farm on All Fools' Day:

> Ay, the great Count Horold!
> His chamberpots are steel and gold,
> And his concubines untold
> Tell they may who be bold,
> Not I . . .

That song had had many verses more: Cleito remembered them now, blushing, and wished she could forget. That was one minstrel—Will the Wanderer—who might yet lose his skin: he had pointedly "not" told a great many of the Count's amorous exploits—exploits which were, of course, common whispers among the people of Westron, but what may be whispered may not always be sung.

And now the "great Count Horold" was looking at her.

Count Horold saw a pretty subject-girl in the green-and-white tunic of a Westrian farm lass. Her sabbat necklace of linked rings was of cheap aluminum, not costly steel or dural, and her sandals were rough and plain too. But she had fine wavy black hair, a fair skin, and very blue eyes.

A blue-eyed maid: he thought. That's a rare one. She is of the old breed, then . . . .

In the ten centuries since the world began, fair blue-eyed people had been steadily disappearing from the population. Dextra's climate was unkind to them: the eternal cloud glare burned their skins and strained their eyes. And if they were on the tall side (as this pretty maid was), the gravity was cruel to them also.

Count Horold smiled. Poor little farm wench, he said to

himself: she is too fine and rare for such a life. Well, there is a remedy for that . . . .

Cleito had turned away, whispering to her cousin Alis. Alis Carver was black-eyed and golden-brown-skinned, a good-looking but more typical girl of Atlantis. Her necklace was of dural, with one large genuine steel ring glinting between her breasts.

"What nonsense, Cleity! Of course he's not looking at you. He was just gazing at the Cathedral front."

"They're calling Uncle Luke over now," said Cleito, her mouth dry.

Alis looked intrigued as her father moved over, bowing low as he approached the Palace party. Her mother, Rhoda, turned to her daughter excitedly.

"I do believe, Alis, the Count was eyeing you! Yes, see, he is still looking our way. My dear, my dear, you may be a made woman yet. I'm so glad now we didn't arrange that marriage for you with old Farmer Hyden."

Cleito was praying: Let it be Alis. Dear goddess, let it be Alis!

The men's conference was now over; the Count's party rode on toward the Cathedral, and Luke Carver returned to his womenfolk. He seemed excited, but also put out.

"You must go home without me for a while, my dears," he said, fidgeting with his doublet. "I am commanded to attend the Count's dinner at the Palace—"

"You, dine at the Palace!" exclaimed his wife, astonished and triumphant.

"Yes, well, the Count has certain matters he wishes to discuss with me—I mean, his chamberlains will discuss with me, and then—then you will *all* pay a visit to the Palace."

"Father," said Alis eagerly, "did you tell them I'm not yet seventeen? But still virgin?"

Luke looked uncomfortable.

"No, no," he said, then turned his head aside, avoiding his wife's eye. "His Highness asked me—about Cleito."

Cleito felt the world spin before her eyes, and the voices of her relations became a senseless chattering. When she had recovered herself, Luke Carver was marching away across the stone-flagged square.

"Come," said Aunt Rhoda grimly. "We are to return to the farm, and then wait." She seemed to consider, and then her manner altered. "Cleito, my dear child," she said softly, almost wheedling, "if the Goddess is being gracious to you, I hope you will not forget your own kinsfolk, who have brought you up and looked after you so well all these years since your poor mother died...."

As they walked through the narrow cobbled streets toward the inn where their mounts were stabled, Cleito could hear with her inner ear the minstrel's song:

> Ay, the great Count Horold!
> Every whore he knows of old,
> And his girls, their charms are sold—
> So they say who make so bold,
> Not I...

At the Inn of the Three Tubolias they picked up their hexips, the six-legged Dextran animals which served as horse or ass to the human colonists. The beasts were in the charge of other native creatures—a couple of faun servants. Indeed, there were many fauns going about their business at the inn. Mahu and Modo were typical specimens. They were a little shorter than Cleito, even when they stood fully erect, which for a faun meant standing on tiptoe, since the natural gait of these little humanoids was digitigrade, like a cat's. They had strong pads under the balls of their bare feet, and only four toes and four fingers; both feet and hands were long and slim. They were *green*—green-skinned, with thick blue head hair and thinner blue fur on their legs. Their ears were pointed, their eyes a little slanted, their irises violet. Some humans affected to find the triangular faun face ugly, but Cleito, who had grown up among them, had always thought them beautiful in their strange unhuman way. Mahu and Modo were identical twins (fauns always came in twins), and they were her old friends—almost.

With fauns, there was always a barrier that one could not cross, a strangeness that had to do with the strange flesh of which they were composed. In the old stories, this barrier was called "the wall between left and right." *Left* meant human, honorable, invader: *right* meant Dextran, humble, native. Even the poorest and most wretched *human* subject-person in Atlantis, nay in all the world, would have to be honorable in comparison to a *faun*. And even if, through a miracle of condescension, a human should sit down at the same table with fauns, he could never eat the same food. Fauns could eat only of the blue and purple vegetation native to Dextra; humans could eat only of Invader plants and animals. The exceptions to this rule were minor, and disagreeable. Cleito had several times had to eat native Golden Apples—that was a stock form of punishment for Westrian farm children, a sort of mild poisoning.

"Mahu," said Aunt Rhoda, "you will stay here with Master's hexip. He is dining at the Palace."

Mahu should have been impressed by this grand announcement. But Cleito noticed that he had not untied the third hexip, while his brother had come forward at once to meet them with the other two. Now Mahu nodded, his strange eyes no wider.

"I will stay, Mistress," he said. "Indeed, I guessed that the Maister would tarry."

He spoke in the usual throaty voice and quaint English of the fauns, and what he said was typical too. The fauns' accent was due to their throat and mouth structure: by human standards, they had long tongues. Their odd English was due to a kind of imprinting. Back in the sixth century, they had been taught the invaders' language—their only language—by a whimsical poet who had used Elizabethan play scripts as teaching materials. Their flair for anticipating their masters' wishes was an unexplained native ability.

Some folk believed that they had second sight, or at least ways of communicating with each other that went beyond words. It was at least true that they seldom spoke to each other unless a human was taking part in the conversation too. This sort of thing might have been frightening, except that hundreds of years of experience had convinced all humans that fauns were no threat to their dominance of the planet. They were happy to be servants and nothing else. They even submitted cheerfully to being bought and sold—not as slaves, but like livestock, domestic animals.

Like domestic animals, they did not form stable pairs between the sexes.

Modo now helped Aunt Rhoda to mount her hexip, and the two girls clambered onto theirs. The womenfolk all rode side saddle, following Westrian custom; Cleito was perched on her animal's second waist, behind Alis. And now they moved out of the courtyard of the inn, into a main thoroughfare of the city. This was a cobbled street, not very wide, leading to the West Gate. On either side rose city houses and shops—all built of wood, and none rising above one story. At one time, hundreds of years earlier, Westron had been different. But all human affairs are subject to change....

So Cleito mused dully as they clattered over the cobbles. She was remembering the sermon she had heard preached that morning by the Chief Witch, Myrto Lee, High Priestess of the Ring Church. Cleito was trained to remember sermons, for Aunt Rhoda often asked her for a paraphrase afterward. It was part of normal education in tenth-century Westria: books were priceless rarities, so memory was cultivated.

"... The Ring," Myrto had said in her sweet clear voice, "in one signification, is Life itself. As a hoop moves, as a circle moves, as the world itself turns, never pausing, never ceasing, so Life goes on. To halt, to be immortal, to remain like a stone, one unchanging thing, that is not the way of Life. That is not the way of the Goddess, who is also Life. The true follower of this Way, the true worshipper of the Goddess, will accept change, not resist it. But pray that your change may be always deosil, in the direction of Life's growth; not widdershins, not perverse. Accept the good change, my brothers and sisters..."

Accept the good change, repeated Cleito to herself. And *my* change now—that thing which is surely coming to me—is *that* good?

Almost at once she found herself thinking of Will the Wanderer again.

That ragged young minstrel had not only sung songs, he had told stories—stories of the youth of the world, which Cleito had found utterly fascinating. Of the time before the Laser Wars, when the Governor of Trinovant had ruled all Atlantis as a mere vassal of the World State or

GenCon; when even the Science Agency had served Gen-Con, and had not yet destroyed the Terror Weapons, or reserved to itself the various Magics such as Lectrissity and Book-printing. And Will had told how in those days, before the Wars broke out in the seventh century, fauns had not been bought and sold; in some provinces they had even been granted *citizen rights* . . . .

"And *citizen* meant a bit more than *subject* now in this Free County," Will had said. "At that time, all the people were equally citizens."

It was at this point that Uncle Luke had driven Will off the farm.

"You'll make us all lose our skins!" he had shouted.

Cleito looked up with a start. This was a time to think of skins! For now they were at the West Gate—a tower, a gateway and a prison, the headquarters of Lord Basil, chief of the Count's spies. And there, above the gate, were the skins.

There had not been any traitors executed lately, so the skins were quite old. But well preserved—the Agency tanners were adepts in that art as in many things else. The cast flayings, realistically stuffed, stood over the gate like so many naked statues. For the sake of decency, the skins of girls or women traitors were not displayed here, but in a certain courtyard of the Palace.

Cleito bowed her head. They were too terrible to look at—even though the faces were quite peaceful. The one at the end was a boy of sixteen—her own age. He had been a Palace page, and had been condemned as a spy for Trinovant, whether truly or not. Rumor had it that his real crime had been a liking for one of the Count's wives or concubines. Well, that would be treason, too; any crime against the Count or his household was treason.

Since the execution of young Rondel, the count had given up employing pages. Now his women were guarded exclusively by fauns—because fauns, contrary to the old myths, felt no desire for human women.

Modo stalked along beside them, leading the girls' hexip through the narrow gateway. He was beautifully graceful with his prancing step, his slim green body covered only from the waist to the thighs by a red loincloth.

Cleito thought, I'd rather be a faun girl than a human

one. Even if I were bought and sold. Nothing seems to touch these dear creatures. And I *am* going to be sold in any case, even though they don't call it that. Alis might like it, to be the Count's thirty-seventh official concubine—not me. I'd rather be a farm beast.

As they moved out from under the city walls onto the muddy road, she also thought: I wonder how it feels when they flay you . . . .

At the waddling trot of the hexips, it took them two hours to reach the farm.

The beaten-earth road wound yellow between fields of young green wheat. For much of the way, it lay along the top of a low ridge, so that they got a wide view left and right—east and west—across the river valley which was the Free County of Westria. To their left at times they glimpsed the broad gray-blue waters of the River Sabrina, and beyond, the green lands rising toward the frontier of Trinovant; to their right, on the western horizon beyond all near green slopes, loomed a high mass of purple—the hills of Evenor, the vast native forest that shielded the Sabrina valley from the Western Ocean, that pirate-haunted sea.

From time to time they passed farms, low buildings in dark blockwood or yellow-white tubolia stems, with tubolia fences and outbuildings. Here there were purple as well as green fields, and meadows of deep-blue grass—native vegetables and grass to feed native livestock. The farms were thronged with fauns and faun-girls peacefully going about their labors, the males quite naked as was usual in the country, the females wearing their faded-red sarongs, cloths which fell from their waists to their ankles. Many of the green-skinned nymphs carried a pair of tiny green babies in a shoulder sling; others had larger babies trotting after them as they worked with their hoes or carried pitchers of water on their heads. There were also their human masters, some newly arrived from sabbat services, or young men who had preferred to stay at home and "supervise"—that is, loaf around, since fauns needed very little or no supervision. All these were people the Carvers knew, more or less, and they waved as the little party plodded up.

THE WILDINGS OF WESTRON 17

Cleito sat, stonily, on her sidesaddle while Aunt Rhoda passed on the exciting news of the Count's favor. And the congratulations ...

"Thank you," she said. "Thank you."

On they trotted, past Crossways and Imber and Faunton and Ringley and Warcoven, hamlets and villages of one-story cottages, each with its small round wooden convenstead. At Tellusford there was also a stone Sword-chapel near a manor house, for Tellusford had been granted by the Count to one of his own knights when he had conquered Westria in the name of his brother of Trinovant some twenty years ago. The religion of the Trinovantian invaders was Swordism, a militant heresy started by the more warlike members of the Ring Church in the early seventh century. Cleito reflected on what Will the Wanderer had made clear to her—that many things in Westria had changed since the conquest. In the time of the old Turner Counts, a man might have only one wife: now the Lords were allowed two, according to Swordist law, and concubines ....

At last they reached their home.

Avonside was named, rather tritely, after the little tributary that fell into the Sabrina a kilometer to the southeast. It was a farm like many others in West Atlantis, a colorful mixture of the two vegetations, with roses mingling with cream-yellow tubolia flowers over the main doorway. It was a rather isolated farm, the village of Ringston lying hidden from it beyond the Avon. It had been Cleito's home as long as she could remember.

They were met in the front yard by her cousin Cadmon, a sturdy youth of eighteen dressed in a rough brown doublet. He was rather handsome in his dark-eyed way, and rather conscious of the fact.

"How was the sabbat?" he asked casually. "The fauns have got dinner ready, Mother."

"Good, good," said Aunt Rhoda, getting down carefully from her hexip with help from Modo. She gave her son a brief hug, and then told him.

Cadmon stared at Cleito, and whistled.

"Hey, Cleity, how d'you like that? You never would give me a kiss, and now it seems your game has paid off. Number thirty-seven, eh?"

"Now, Cadmon," said Aunt Rhoda quickly, "that's no way to talk. Remember, Cleito is going to be a *Court lady* now—"

"How much will we get for her, d'you think, Mother?" said Cadmon.

Rhoda simpered. "Well, I wouldn't like to say. But you know, that time our dear Count went visiting abroad, he paid a *hundred pieces of iron* for that Nordic captive girl, and her eyes were no bluer than our Cleito's."

Cadmon whistled again. "A hundred pieces? Why, if we got that, we could buy that half-kilo field on the other side of the river, and pay for our marriages, and—"

"It *won't* be a hundred pieces," said Alis spitefully, looking at Cleito. "Our dear Count had to bargain for the Nordic girl with foreign pirates. Here, he can fix his own price. We'll be lucky if we get thirty."

"Go and wash now, children," said Aunt Rhoda. "Cleito, after dinner we'll start sprucing you up properly. We don't know when they may come."

Cleito fled.

"Where are you off to?" cried Alis, surprised. "That's not the way to the wash-place!"

"I'm going to the river," said Cleito. "I have to be very thoroughly washed, remember? You can have the wash-place to yourself."

Alis sniffed. "Mind no *people* see you then; don't forget, your charms are bespoken, you mustn't *lower* your *price*."

When Cleito reached the bank of the Avon, there were no people about. The place was not visible from any road, and it was sheltered by thick purple-leaved bushes. She stripped off her necklace and tunic and sandals and stepped naked into the shallow water, then ducked completely under the cool translucent surface. She felt like washing away everything that had happened to her that morning. Under water, she opened her eyes on a dreamy green world.

She thought: O my goddess, if only I could slip away, swim down to the sea, be a mermaid ...

... and for that matter there *were* tales about mermaids: blue-skinned sea-nymphs, sisters of the green faun-

THE WILDINGS OF WESTRON 19

girls, blue girls with webbed fingers and fishtails that sailors had reported at sea.

It was all nonsense, of course. She couldn't live like a mermaid off native fish, which were poisonous to humans. Anyway, whether there were mermaids or not, she couldn't escape. Even if she ran away fast enough to evade the Count's men-at-arms, even if she could find somewhere to eke out her life, she couldn't leave her uncle's family to face the Count's wrath. He probably wouldn't flay them, but he might well ruin them, run them off their farm. She couldn't do that to them, even though she was treated by them as something less than a daughter, and even though Alis was spiteful and Cadmon boorish. No, she would have to stay, and be taken as Number 37.

She had ducked underwater a second time when she saw a dim form approaching through the water—a slim green body moving efficiently with fishlike movements of the long feet. For a second she thought of mermaids; then with a little laugh, she raised her head above the surface.

The faun girl got her footing in the same instant.

"Mistress Cleito," she said, smiling through her tangle of wet blue hair. Instantly her expression changed. "But ye are sad . . ."

"O Melly!" cried Cleito, half sobbing. She threw her arms around the green girl's neck, and buried her face in her blue hair, nuzzling her pointed ears. "Melly, they're going to sell me."

"Sell you? But ye are no nymph, my Mistress, to be marketed like a little faun sister. O, now I mind it: the Count, is't not so?"

"How did you know?" said Cleito, straightening up.

"Oh," said Melissa, smoothing her blue hair with her slim green fingers, "it came presently into my mind; mayhap Modo was minding it at that moment. So: the Count will take you as an Honorable Concubine for some thirty pieces of iron. Well, that is five times more than any man will pay for a faun girl, so ye should be Honorable and honored indeed."

"Oh Melly, don't be silly," said Cleito, with mock anger. Melissa was her best friend, if one could be friends with a farm animal—no, she *was* her best friend, quite simply.

Melissa was a little unusual for a faun, perhaps because her twin had died young, leaving her isolated with a more individual personality. She was two years younger than Cleito chronologically, but about the same age physically, since nymphs matured more quickly. Melissa could be quite witty at times; and now she was obviously trying to cheer her up by getting her to take her trouble lightly. But Cleito could not. "Melly," she went on seriously, "you know men don't buy faun girls for *that* reason."

"No, Mistress?" said Melissa. "It minds me now that sometimes they do. I have a picture of a pretty faun girl at Alvern Manor, for whom her master Sir Hugo paid six pieces last year."

"How *disgusting!*" said Cleito. "Not even the Count, no one's ever said that of him—how could a man—"

"It is *possible*," said Melissa drily. "Not nice for us, but possible."

Cleito looked at the naked nymph. Melissa was shaped very like a human girl, but there were important hidden differences. Cleito knew these facts of Dextran native life very well. Melissa could of course never be impregnated by a human male; and that was the least of it. She had small pseudo-breasts with distinct violet nipples, but these structures were altogether nonfunctional: her true milk glands—three of them—lay in the back of her mouth, in a structure corresponding to the human soft palate. Males also had milkless nipples there. Suckling in Dextran mammals looked very much like kissing.

The false external "breasts" and "nipples" of the native nymphs were a biological mystery, accounted for in that old saga the Tale of the Turners by the notion that they were there merely to please the eyes of humans—a sort of symbiotic adaptation. Once, according to the saga, nymphs and fauns had been very far from human-looking, but they had been altered to suit human taste by some magic power in an Eastern jungle. If that were true, thought Cleito as she gazed at Melissa, the Power had certainly done a good job.

Melissa had a navel—a functional one, very human-looking—and below this on her lower abdomen a vertical blue line, just visible against her green skin. For this organ most human women would have given all the pieces of iron they possessed. For when Melissa's time came to give birth to her sets of twins, her belly would open up like a pea pod, and out would come the little green babies with no fuss and not the least pain. Below the birth organ was a humanoid vagina but no hymen—nymphs have no physical virginity—and no urinary tract, for nymphs excrete only through one opening behind. Perhaps for this reason, they do not associate sex with dirt, or feel any compulsion to hide their sexual parts.

Also, Cleito knew, their mechanism of sexual arousal was very different from the human. It had very little to do with the vagina, and very much to do with the mouth. All this Melissa had explained to her long ago with the utmost frankness, for nymphs are nicely shameless, and do not mind discussing their love lives with their friends.

"Oh, Melly!" sighed Cleito. "How I wish I were you, or your sister. So many fewer troubles!"

Melissa gave a throaty little laugh.

"Mayhap you will be a nymph in your next life, Missy Cleito, and then, if I am with ye, we may discuss whether ye have changed your mind. But come now, what are we to do about this trouble of yours? It seems you do not like your honorable master-to-be? Nay, I see you do not. Well, it is hard to avoid him, seeing he is the master of everybody in this Free County; but at least I may be able to help you bear your grief. By my advice, you might put it into Mistress Rhoda's head that you need a lady's maid to go with you to the Palace. You know that is customary in the city. Well, I think I could serve."

"O, Melly, would you?" said Cleito, gripping her friend's green shoulders, and smiling with sudden joy.

"Nay, marry would I, and so *must* I too, if I am commanded by my owners."

Cleito flung her arms round Melissa's neck; and her shapely white breasts gently squeezed her friend's little green imitations.

"Oh, Melly," she said, tossing her black hair out of her eyes, "if you stay with me, I think I can bear his mere lust."

"Nay, that will not trouble you much after a while," said Melissa drily. "Once his first fancy is past, what with thirty-six other girls and two wives and whatnot else, you'll be lucky to have any lust to *suffer* . . . ."

The city of Westron is roughly circular in plan, with the eastern half tucked into a meander of the Sabrina River. The Count's palace occupies the northeast sector: it was formerly the University, when universities existed on Dextra before the seventh-century Laser Wars. At the south end of the city, where the meander straightens out and the city walls begin to confront the open plain, there rises the citadel-monastery of the Science Agency. The Count's palace is a spacious, gracious set of buildings in mellow sandstone; the Agency hold is a grim huddle of dark rock. But unlike every other building in Westron, including the Palace, the Agency is surmounted by a radio mast, and a hedgerow of windpumps and a gleaming tower of solar cells: for this is a place of power and knowledge forbidden to layfolk—indeed, forbidden also to secular clergy, by the strict Covenant that ended the Laser Wars.

Yet secular clergy did sometimes visit the Agency, especially under cover of night. Thus it was, that spring sabbat evening, that two people were gathered in a little room overlooking the river. The night was dark, for though the clouds were merely thin high cirrus, not a single moon was up. The room was lit by a dim red electric strip, which barely showed the outlines of the faces. But the two who were met there that night hardly needed even that much light to read each other's thoughts.

"So," said Ambrose Anders, the Chief Agent, "he is still suspicious of the Church of the Ring, Myrto? I thought you had been lying low."

"We've been groveling," said the shadowy woman in her beautifully musical voice. "But yes, he is still suspicious. He wants us to give up half our Cathedral to his Sword Cult. I suppose we'll have to. Damned savage heretics! But Goddess knows, the Ring is mightier than the Sword—and the Ring has its own methods of winning a game. Ambrose, my dear, do you know that the Count is about to take a new concubine?"

The Agent laughed softly. "Of course; my green-skinned servants have informed me already, as usual. I suppose yours told you, my dear Chief Witch?"

"Yes," said Myrto. "Ambrose, they say she is a nice girl, and a devout worshipper of the Goddess."

"Then I hope you will contact her at once. If possible, *before* . . ."

"Leave that to me," said the Chief Witch. "Even a Swordist like our noble Count is sure to defer to our superior aura in matters of love. The auspicious day, you know . . ."

"Friday would be safe," said Ambrose. "Astrologically impeccable, and not too far ahead to make his lust too impatient. When will she be here?"

"Tomorrow for certain."

"That gives you three days. Surely you can brief her."

Myrto sighed. "I'll do my best. They surely can't deny me a private ceremony. Oh Goddess, Ambrose, if only she were . . . you know, one of us."

"She's not, I suppose?"

"Not as far as I can tell. Her own name is Dixon, and her relations are Carvers and Smiths and Costellos. If there's any trace of the Blessed Blood, it must be quite far back. I'll have to use only *words*; and I've got to watch those, in the Palace."

"You may have to watch those here, too," said the Agent, looking around. "This room is quite safe still—my fauns check it every day to make sure the Physicists haven't slipped something in. Quite a few of them are *his* men now, you know. Thank the Convenant for the Separation of Disciplines! We've kept them out of the Biology Courtyards so far. The worst is that now *he* is putting forward candidates for *Biology*. We've managed to turn them down so far, but it's getting awkward. I'm sure he doesn't suspect our *real* objection, but . . . If he does find someone suitable, and invokes the Covenant, then I'll have no option but to admit him."

"Blessed be!" said the Chief Witch, reaching forward to touch Ambrose's hand. "Then there won't be any respite for those poor victims."

"Respite?" said the Chief Agent bitterly. "It's worse than that, Myrto—we may have to stop doing it *at all*— and get rid of what we use."

Myrto contemplated, appalled. "Ambrose—" she began.

"No more words now," he said. "We had better practice. We may have to do without speech altogether one day."

Their conversation continued—but now no auditory device could have reported them to the Count's spies.

Chapter
TWO

They came for Cleito on Tuesday at high dawn—the time when all colors are clear, and the eternal clouds are bright in the east. They were a strong mounted guard in the Count's crimson surcoats, led by a knight in costly dural armor. This man handed Cleito over at once to an elderly faun named Narses, the Count's Second Chamberlain. Narses, astonishingly, was dressed like a man in doublet and hose—hose which ended at his ankles leaving his feet bare, since no one had ever invented shoes which would fit a faun. He also wore a dural chain-of-office, a collar of linked H's, symbol of the dynasty of Harkness. Narses helped Cleito up into the forward saddle of a sturdy hexip, and then, to her surprise, mounted behind her and took the long reins.

"Ay, there be some fauns that *do* ride," said Narses gravely, "those that are high in the Court's favor, like myself and my brother Nemon, who is First Chamberlain. My lord the Count trusts us better than some humans—but let that pass. 'Tis my office, my lady, to have charge of you and to prepare you for the honor which is in store for you. Fear nothing, I have experience in these matters, and I will take gentle care of you. And you will be allowed to see your family, of course, both before your handfasting and after."

He looked down at Melissa trotting demurely along beside them, her naturally well padded bare tiptoes keeping up easily with the waddle of the hexip: and beyond her at Rhoda and Alis, who were sharing another strong steed.

He continued: "You will not lack for company where you are going, dear lady."

Narses had spoken gently enough, but Cleito was not in a mood to be gentled. "How dear *was* I, in the end?" she said.

"Pardon me, my lady, I do not take your meaning."

"How many pieces did the Count bid? I have not yet been told."

"Forty pieces for you and your maid," said Narses. "It is a great sum; His Highness has never given as much before for a Westrian girl. You have great honor therefor."

"And how much did the Count pay for *you*, Narses, when he bought you?"

"My lady, I was never bought, I was born in the palace in the old Count's time before the Conquest. But you must not speak so: you are a human girl, not an animal like me! We do not have human slavery in Westria. His Highness has not bought you, he has accepted you from your family and given them a present as a mark of his favor."

"Oh yes, that makes a *big* difference," said Cleito. "And—after I am handfasted, since I am not a slave, will I be allowed to leave the Palace sometimes to visit my friends?"

"Unfortunately not. But your friends can visit you—your women friends, that is, under proper supervision."

"But *this* can't visit me," said Cleito waving at the countryside, her voice almost breaking. It was another beautiful day, with only high cirrus: the golden aura of the almost visible sun suffused the whole Sabrina valley from the purple hills of Evenor to the green Easter Heights. "Narses," she said, mastering herself, "I have always been a country girl."

"There are spacious gardens in the Palace, my lady. And, if you like, I can find you a cell overlooking the river."

"A *cell?*" gasped Cleito, horrified.

Narses grasped her shoulder reassuringly and smiled. "They are not bad. It is merely our name for the Minor Ladies' bedchambers. There will be a soft bed for you and a pallet for your maid, and fine carpets, and a chest full of lovely cloaks and tunics and jewels—"

"And bars on the windows?"

Narses gazed at her gravely, then slowly nodded his head.

When they reached the Palace, Cleito was separated from Rhoda and Alis. Narses helped her to dismount in one of the outer courtyards, then led her and Melissa through colonnades and passages. These parts of the Palace were moderately thronged with courtiers and human stewarts and faun servants. It was a world which Cleito had never known before, and in other circumstances it might have been fascinating. The courtiers were magnificently dressed, and many of the fauns wore clothes in imitation of humans. Some stood beside doorways like guards, carrying tubolia-wood pikes, and these all wore strange headpieces, blue furry caps from which sprouted a pair of artificial horns.

"Why—" began Cleito.

Narses explained. "It is a witty fancy of His Highness, my lady. In old legends, fauns are pictured as having natural horns. Now, we really do not have them, so our masters has remedied the deficiency of nature."

"And that's a witty fancy? Narses, I like you the way you are."

The courtiers and the lackeys all stood aside as they passed by, and they bowed low to Cleito.

I wonder how long *that* will last, she thought. From what she had heard, concubines who had ceased to please the Count quickly forfeited such marks of respect—though they were never returned to their families.

At last they came to a staircase, a real double flight of stone stairs leading to an upper floor.

"I will call for a litter," said Narses, and clapped his hands.

"I'm sure I can climb those," said Cleito, looking at the stairs. "There are a few steps outside the Cathedral, and I've always managed those all right. And once on our farm I even climbed a tree."

"You must not mention such things," said Narses, upset. "Climbing *anything* is not ladylike!"

"Won't I have to climb into the Count's bed? He has a high one, I'm told."

"You will be carried into that," said Narses. "And we will carry you now. Please you to step in."

The litter rose, swaying on the backs of six strong young fauns; and up the stairs they went, Narses and Melissa walking beside. Cleito hoped her weight did not strain her bearers too terribly. She recalled one of the stories of Will the Wanderer, a tale of old Tellus, a mad romance about buildings with dozens of floors, one above the other, buildings with beams of *steel*, as in a fairy tale. Well, there had been no fauns on Tellus, so if those lords and ladies had used litters, they'd have had to be carried by other *humans* ... but of course, everything had weighed less there—"only four-fifths as much," Will had said.

Will ... she wondered what had happened to him. A nice young man, about twenty years old, with brown eyes and brown hair. They called him a Wilding—at least Uncle Luke did—but that was only fanciful abuse. Wildings were a legend, nothing more. For who could live in the virgin purple forest, except the odd wild faun? Will was just a strolling minstrel, ragged and barefoot. She had liked him, but of course they could never ... her uncle would have had a fit ... and yet Will *had* looked at her once or twice as though he liked what he saw, and she hadn't minded being liked by him.

She shook her head, as if to clear it of fancies. All that was over now, in any case.

Her room in the Corridor of Minor Ladies was as Narses had described it. The single barred window looked out over the broad waters of the Sabrina and the white sails of passing rivercraft. The room itself held more luxuries than Cleito was used to, including a stone space in one corner where an aluminum spout came through the wall.

"It's for washing," said Narses. "Take off your clothes and stand under it, and I will show you."

Cleito had no shame about stripping in front of fauns—long experience had taught her that this meant nothing to them. She gave her tunic and sandals to Melissa, and stood obediently where Narses directed. Then she watched as he turned an oddly shaped handle on the wall, and—miracle! Water flowed out of the spout through dozens of little holes and rained down on her body.

"It's called a shower," said Narses, smiling. "All the Palace has this marvelous system—our maids do not have to carry many pitchers. 'Tis thanks to the wizardry of the Agency. Here, my lady, try this *soap*."

"Soap?" said Cleito, bewildered, taking the block.

"You rub it on yourself," explained Narses. "Mix it with the water."

"Oh!" said Cleito, rubbing. It smelled marvelous.

"See the delights of Palace life?" said Narses. "There are others, too—feasting and wine and bright *lectric* lamps that burn Agency magic."

"Can Melissa try this too?" asked Cleito, letting the sweet-smelling water run off her body.

Narses looked dubiously at the faun girl, then quickly nodded. "I make no objection," he said, "though there be others who might."

Melissa kissed Narses on the palm of his right hand, then stripped off her sarong and stepped under the shower beside Cleito.

"Nice, nice," said Cleito after a while. "But really, we're more used to bathing in a stream, and there you have more room to move."

"We have wide bathing pools too," said Narses. "There you can bathe, even swim a little, with the other Court ladies in a yard with a marble fountain. No man comes there but my master and yours, to gaze sometimes upon his three dozen beauties. Now, Mistress Cleito, dry yourself. And answer me truthfully: are ye yet a maid?"

Cleito nodded.

"That is well," said Narses, "else would your uncle have to pay dear for his lying to the Count. But I must be sure, girl: you understand?"

"I understand," said Cleito, and submitted. She had been expecting this, and Narses was gentle and did not humiliate her in his quick examination.

"Well," said the Chamberlain, stepping back, *"that* is a relief."

Over the next three days Cleito was bathed, scented, painted, dressed, undressed and instructed in all the arts and graces necessary to a young novice concubine. Narses and a couple of faun assistants painted her fingernails and toenails crimson, the color of the Count's banner and livery, and they plucked her eyebrows until they were thin black lines. They put up her hair in a complicated fashion and bound it into place with strings of real pearls from Tethys Sea. Cleito reckoned that her new jewels and bracelets and necklace cost about as much as she did herself.

She did not mind the dressing-up particularly. It was some of the training which made her ashamed. She was being taught to deliver herself like a parcel into her master's arms—a parcel which unwrapped itself, as seductively as possible. She feared that the training might go even further—but no: Narses told her that her more intimate education would be undertaken by the Count himself.

"He delights in teaching beginners everything that is necessary in that way," said the old faun.

At this stage, she had very little contact with the Count's other women. A guard of young faun pike-bearers was always stationed at her door, and she was carefully escorted whenever she left her room, which was not often. Once, though, on her first evening in the Palace, when the mellow-shaded *lectric* lamp in the corner had just come on, and she and Melissa were marveling at the steady glow, a girl's face peered in past the heavy curtain of the doorway.

She was a tall girl with light-brown, almost yellowish hair and blue eyes. She wore, apparently, nothing but a dark-red cloak suspended from one shoulder by a roughly tied knot.

"So—you're the new one," she said, with just a hint of a strange lilting accent. "Do you mind if I come in? I'll leave my cloak outside if you're afraid."

"Afraid?" said Cleito, astonished. "Of what? Who *are* you?"

"I'm Estrild," said the girl. "Number twenty at present—I have four years' seniority. I am not carrying any dagger under my cloak; your fauns have searched me thoroughly, and even taken away my shoulder-brooch."

"Come in," said Cleito, "and keep your cloak." She paused. "Do I really have to fear that someone might stab me?"

"Not very likely," admitted Estrild, seating herself gracefully on a cushioned mat. "Poison is our favorite weapon here." She smiled. "How about a little pact, Cleito? If you promise never to poison me, I promise never to poison you."

"Of *course*," said Cleito. "What kind of place *is* this?"

"A nest of quarreling bored she-sphinxes," said Estrild. "But I guess it's better than Akhor, so I'm not sorry the Count bought me away from there."

"You were taken by Akhorian pirates?" said Cleito, horrified. "I thought you were from Nordica. Akhor is south."

"They go anywhere," said the fair-haired girl. "They made a shore raid on my village. Killed all the men. I wished that they had killed me too—it is not nice at all to be a slave to those Saintly ruffians! They behave like pigs to women, and what's nearly worse, they are pious about it—everything they do they justify from their filthy old Scriptures. This Count's palace is at least better than *that*."

"Oh, poor distressful lady," said Melissa suddenly, "wouldn't you like to go home?"

"Home?" said Estrild, and laughed shortly. "I have no home—the Akhorians saw to that. This is my home now, I suppose. Cleito, let us be friends, not rivals. I would like to give you some advice."

Estrild's advice soon had Cleito blushing.

"I'd rather not talk about it," she said. "But you, Estrild, you say he is not interested in you now. What do you do now to pass your time?"

Estrild began: "Well, fauns are no good, so . . . ."

Cleito was amazed, and horrified. She had come across nothing like this in the country.

"With other *women?*" she breathed. "How could you?"

"What else is there?" said Estrild, yawning. "Of course I would prefer men. Before he got rid of those pages, there was always a dangerous hope. Now, only women. God and Goddess, Cleito, you had better learn to please His Highness . . . ."

On Thursday morning she was taken to bathe in the Court of the Fountains, but when she got there with Narses and the guards and Melissa, she found the place empty.

"It has been cleared for you," said Narses. "Things will be different when the Count has taken you. Till then you are precious. Undress now, my lady—in *that* way, the way you have been taught."

Cleito raised her newly elegant eyebrows, surveyed the two-story buildings about the courtyard, then shrugged. There were no windows, and no one about, so there were only fauns to watch her performance. She decided to do her best so as to please her anxious teacher. Slowly, langorously, she undid the shoulder-knot of her flame-colored robe, and let it slip off her; then unwound the semi-transparent sari-like underwrap. Lastly she put her hands to her waist, untwisted the folds of her gorgeously patterned sarong, and slowly revealed her nakedness.

A bright-yellow tubolia flower fell on the flagstones in front of her feet, the petals brushing her crimson toenails. From the upper story of the nearest building came the sound of applause. A stone slab had slid aside, and there was the Count, in doublet, cloak and diadem, with faun faces beside him.

"Bravo, bravo!" he cried, beaming. "Mistress Cleito, well done. Your perfections are even as they have been described by Narses, and your performance was superb. Alas, great princes must be slaves to custom, else I would not wait another minute ... but as it is, another thirty hours must separate us, my sweet one. Till then—ah, I cannot bear any more such torture."

He flung out a whole armful of flowers, and then the stone slab closed and hid him and his retinue.

Cleito had stood as if paralyzed all the while. Then she turned to Narses.

"You *knew!*"

"My lady, it was necessary," said the faun apologetically. "You are such a shy one."

"I knew too," said Melissa, gathering up the flowers. "What of it? Missy Cleito, if you are playing this game at all, it is necessary to play it well."

She received the same advice that evening from Myrto, the Chief Witch of Westron.

Myrto had met her in the private chapel reserved for those few members of the Count's court who professed the

THE WILDINGS OF WESTRON 33

faith of the Ring. They had the room to themselves, and Myrto first performed a brief service of prayer to the Goddess of a Thousand Names, with Cleito acting as her Maiden. When the ritual Circle had been banished, Cleito sat crosslegged on the ground before Myrto on her Priestess's throne.

Myrto Lee was a handsome woman of some thirty years, rather dark-skinned with very black eyes and broad cheekbones. Her hair was like a waterfall of night.

"Look now into my eyes," she said.

Cleito stared until she seemed to be drowning in those pools of darkness. Then Myrto said:

"I have seen into your eyes too, my child-deep, deep. I know now that I am in the presence of a future Countess of Westron."

Cleito cried out: "Impossible! He wouldn't—he never does—"

"With the Goddess," said Myrto, "all things are possible. Now, listen: you must act as follows . . . ."

"Well," said Cleito tremulously, after several minutes, "I will try, Myrto. But I must say, I can never *love* him. The things he has done—he's cruel, surely. All those *executions*." And she shuddered.

"I will tell you one thing," said Myrto slowly. "There would have been no flayings if it had not been for Ambrose, the Chief Agent."

"What?"

"Before the present Count conquered Westron, in the time of the Turner dynasty, the penalty for treason was simply beheading—and even that was very seldom invoked. After the Conquest, there were naturally a lot of traitors. Well, Ambrose was already Chief Agent in those days, and he persuaded the Count to change the penalty."

"How horrible!" shuddered Cleito. "I did not know the Agent was so wicked. I did not think the Agency cared about such matters."

"They use the bodies," said Myrto, "for scientific purposes, you understand: half the Templars in the Westron Agency are biologists. They perform the whole execution themselves, and merely hand over the skin to the Count as proof that the criminal is dead. Recently, Ambrose has been pressing the Count to make all executions in Westron flayings; he says he can use more bodies now in his research."

"O Goddess!" sobbed Cleito. "How can the clouds and the earth see such things? I feel unclean even thinking about them—because we are all kin, all we children of the First Landers, and so what Ambrose has done, I have done too, in a way."

"My child," said Myrto, "your feelings do you credit. Indeed, you are right. There is a vileness in the human race which will keep breaking out. The First Hundred who landed in this world nearly a thousand years ago—they were picked people, the best of our kind, chosen to be the founders of a new world. And for many generations their descendants lived together in reasonable amity. But then, the fatal itch to conquer . . . There were those who called themselves Lordists or Saints, and they mostly wished to destroy all the native life of this planet. In the end they quarrelled with the moderates, people like those who founded our own Ring Church: and so came the Wars, three hundred years ago. Nine out of ten humans were slaughtered then by the beams of death, and the world broke up into little princedoms. Now our human wickedness emerges openly, but not dangerously as long as the Agency remains to prevent the spread of inventions. This is the human condition that we must live with: all power will be abused, unless our race is altered."

"Oh," said Cleito, "I wish we could all turn into fauns! *They* don't commit crimes, *they* don't flay each other, *they* don't make slaves of each other or of us."

"Softly, softly, my dear," said the Chief Witch, leaning forward and stroking Cleito's hair. "The fauns indeed are a lovely race, and dear to the Goddess; but we need not despair of humanity either. Your very horror shows that. If we were utterly evil, we would not even know it. Evil indeed is the shadow of goodness, as you learned in coven-school: for goodness to exist, evil must exist also. But there are degrees in all things, and it is not *necessary* that the world should be as evil as it is now. Therefore the struggle is worth carrying on; and therefore I wish to enlist you on the right side. We must work by craft, dear Cleito, Ring against Sword. . . ."

Chapter
THREE

Next morning Cleito awoke to find Melissa kneeling by her bed. Instantly she remembered that it was Friday. She flung herself into the faun girl's arms.

After a while, Melissa drew back, and said, "Mistress, they are coming for us, I think."

"The Count?" whispered Cleito.

"Nay, not he, that will not be till after this evening's feast, as ye should know. But Narses, I think, and his twin Nemon, the First Chamberlain. Prepare yourself: it is something fearsome, for there is fear in their hearts."

Cleito put on a plain tunic, and then the fauns arrived. She learned that she was going to be taken on a little tour of a part of the Palace.

Nemon was so like his brother that it would have been difficult to tell them apart except for their different insignia: the First Chamberlain wore a double neck chain. He said, "There is something that we show to every new woman. It is by the Count's orders. Come, girl."

Her litter went up another staircase, so that they were now in one of the highest towers of the Palace. The litter bearers put down their burden in a narrow antechamber, and Cleito stepped out through an archway into an old dusty courtyard. The stonework here was neglected and in places crumbling, but she had no eyes for that. She had already looked up and glimpsed the burden of the walls.

Her heart missed a beat. Or rather, she felt that it had stopped altogether, that she was now moving into the world of the dead between incarnations. For there were lifeless bodies poised above her, arms outspread as though flying. But as her vision cleared, she saw that they were suspended against the stones, motionless, trussed with ropes, crucified with wooden pegs, all naked.

It was like the traitors of Westgate, with one difference: these traitors were women.

Some were quite young, girls of her own age, black-haired and honey-skinned, with staring open black eyes—for the taxidermists of the Agency were superb in their craft. The Count had here another seraglio, the beauties of yesteryear whose eternal summer would not fade. Indeed, he must have thrown away the skins of the old and ugly female traitors, for all these naked dead fliers were young and beautiful.

Cleito thought she had reached the ultimate of horror, when in turning she caught sight of a very small figure on the wall. An exception: this was the stuffed skin and face of a small boy, perhaps no more than two years old at death. His hair was brown, and the taxidermist had given him brown glass eyes.

"What—what—?" she said, turning to the fauns.

"Prince Elric," said Nemon tonelessly. "He was the only member of the previous ruling family to survive the massacre—I mean the battle—when the Count conquered Westron twenty years ago. His nurse took refuge with the boy in the Agency citadel; but my lord Ambrose decided, in the interests of stable government, that the boy could not live; and so presently he handed over his skin."

Melissa slipped her arms around Cleito's waist and shoulders, silently comforting her. Cleito was wondering if she could possibly by herself devise a curse that would injure Ambrose, when another party stepped into the courtyard. First came a man in a red-and-black doublet, a man of some thirty years, very dark, with a scar on one cheek, and a hard mouth and intent eyes; then a band of faun lackeys; then the Count, with more fauns behind him. Count Horold was holding a strange object in his hands.

"Ah, my sweet Cleito," he said, smiling at her. "Admiring some of your predecessors, I see. Mind you, only naughty girls end up here—don't they, Basil?—and you will be in no such danger, I'm sure. But look now, my sweet, here is something much more remarkable."

He held up the instrument in his hands. It was of metal, black, shiny and apparently heavy though not very big: a tube with a hand grip attached below it.

"I found it while poking about in one of the empty rooms of this tower," said the Count. "It was buried in a niche behind some old stones. I think it had lain there for three hundred years, just waiting for me to find it. I'm glad," he said, casting a quick glance at the lord Basil, "that it was my own hand that came to it first. I may say it is in beautiful condition, and one of the old books in my library has shown me how to use it. Let me see ... ah yes, that little fellow there. He'd be no loss, I think."

The Count raised the black tube until the end pointed at the little boy-wraith on the wall. Then his finger tightened.

A deep hole appeared in the stonework. The Count moved his hand slightly from left to right, and the small body was cut in half at the waist. The lower portion fell at once to the flagstone of the yard floor.

"Not very pretty like that, is he?" said the Count, and pressed again, moving his hand in a circle. The rest of the body disappeared in fragments, and the stone wall looked as though it had been struck by a shower of meteorites. The air seemed to be full of burned particles.

"The trouble is," said the Count, "the power is really enormous. I could cut down the whole tower if I wanted to." He pushed a lever on the black handle. "There," he said, relaxing. "It's safe now." He laughed. "But now, let no enemies of Westria think to engage Count Horold in informal battles!"

Cleito gazed steadily at her master and lover-to-be. She remembered what she had promised Myrto.

Could she go through with it? Surely, surely *anything*, any personal shame would be justified if it helped the opposition to the Count of Westron—who now commanded one of the Terror Weapons which had nearly destroyed the world.

It was justified; but that did not make it easy to do.

It was full night, and yet the banqueting hall was splendid with magic Agency lighting. Half-hidden yellow lamps threw artificial auras on the ceiling of black beams and pale tubolia-wood panels; other redder *lectric* torches were held like spears, their butts to the floor, their imitation flames on high, by horn-capped fauns. These attendants, all in red doublets with the white Sword-cross, the Count's device, on their breasts, lined the walls and guarded the black wooden stairs that led to the Count's apartments.

The room was filled with tables, and the tables were occupied by feasters: the Count's barons, knights, burgesses, indeed all the notables of Westria. At the High table on the supreme dais sat the Count with his two wives and their sons, the princes Steelmon and Ferizel. At the bottom of the hall, at some very low tables, sat the non-noble subjects, the wealthy burghers and the dignitaries of the Churches and the Agency. Further up were the Swordist knights and barons, with the Lord Basil, the Count's bastard brother and head of his secret service, at their highest table. At the sides of the hall, between the tables and the faun torchbearers, there crouched a number of minstrels with lutes, the court poets in their singing robes at the top end of the hall, the humbler bards below beside the burgesses.

Everyone was dressed in their most expensive clothes: there was much flashing of jewels, and of costly dural and steel. Cleito wore a loose crimson robe that fell from a sparkling but heavy steel brooch on her left shoulder, leaving her right shoulder bare. She was seated at a small table in solitary splendor, just below the Count's table on a slightly lower dais, so placed that all the feasters could see her perfectly. She could sense their various feelings very easily.

She knew that the barons and knights were admiring the whiteness of her skin, the blueness of her eyes, the blackness of her hair, and that every man of them was wishing himself in the Count's place. She guessed that the Countesses were glaring at her from behind, and the Princes regarding her with suspicion mingled with frustrated adolescent lust. At a couple of side tables a little below hers, she could see most of the thirty-six other concubines. Estrild was there—one friendly face; all the others seemed to be wishing that looks carried poison.

O Goddess, she said to herself, give me courage. Must they make this spectacle of me?

She was the Count's latest trophy, and therefore she

must be displayed. Like an animal newly slain in a hunt—and perhaps they would have her head on a wall after, nay her whole skin too. She was very near fainting. It was only the comfort of Melissa, her table attendant, squatting by her side and occasionally caressing her ankle, that gave her courage to endure.

The "handfasting" had been not at all like a marriage ceremony—much simpler and over more quickly. The Carver family had been summoned up from the lower end of the hall, and her Uncle Luke, with many low bows, had placed her hands within those of the Count. The Count had then pushed over each of her hands a precious steel bracelet engraved with his Sword badge—and thus she had become his official concubine, number 37. The ceremony would be sealed in her flesh very soon now, in fact as soon as the Count had drunk the customary number of toasts.

It would surely be a relief to get it over with . . . .

If only they would give her something to drink! Some strong wine, to deaden her sensations. But the Count had sent her only one small cup by way of a pledge, and now she was getting only fruit juices. Narses had told her that her master did not like his girls to smell of wine: he preferred them alert, precise in their movements, aware of what they were doing and what was being done to them.

Everything she ate or drank was being tasted first by the Senior Concubine, Number One, a handsome woman of some thirty years who looked at her as though she would gladly give her own life to poison Cleito also. A pleasant life I shall have here, thought Cleito. And Alis *envied* me this! I suppose she still does . . . .

She looked down at dear green-skinned Melissa. Oh, she thought, if only I could change places with her. I'd rather be a real slave—less than a slave, an *animal*. But that would be unfair to Melissa, to wish her *this* . . . .

Time was wearing on now, and the feast was losing some of its formality as the guests became flushed and emboldened with wine. Soon the Count would drink the parting cup, and then . . . But now people were coming up, lords and notables, to bow to the Count and congratulate him. That man in the green cowled robe, with the white hair . . . Very calm features, very strange black eyes . . .

" 'Tis the Lord Ambrose, the Chief Agent," whispered Melissa.

Cleito's heart gave a lurch. Impossible! But it was so—this was the Chief Agent, that creature of hideous science so much more wicked in his cold cruelty than the Count himself.

Ambrose was talking to the Count now. It was quite impossible to hear what he was saying, in all the hubbub; but the Count's face had darkened. He replied to Ambrose in a barely controlled snarl. Ambrose gazed at him steadily for a moment, then said a couple of calm words, bowed and withdrew.

"I am thinking, mistress," whispered Melissa, "that the Lord Ambrose knows of the Count's dreadful weapon."

"Oh yes," said Cleito dully. "Any such thing must be handed over to the Agency to be destroyed—that is part of the Covenant. If Ambrose asked for that, then I think I know what the Count's answer was. I don't think it matters—if the Agency is wicked too, it doesn't matter who has the weapon."

The Count was playing with a sphinx, one of the purple-furred flying cats of Dextra. The small creature sat on his High Table, its wing-skin severely clipped so that it could not fly. As he tickled it under the chin, the Count looked at Cleito. He seemed to have recovered his good humor. He smiled, and gestured to one of the Court poets. The man stalked forward, struck his lute, and sang:

> "Speak to me not of Paradise,
> Elysium, Eden or such lands:
> My only blessed kingdom stands
> Much nearer, and much sweeter lies,
> And here I pay my duty:
> Our best delight
> By day or night
> Is woman's love, and woman's beauty."

"I hope you like my song, Cleito," called the Count, "I composed it myself, in your honor."

Cleito bowed to her master. Melissa whispered:

"I' faith, he lies. The bard's faun servant is putting it into my mind that *his* master wrote it entire."

The singer delivered the second stanza:

> "Tell me not of sweet Tellus' ore,
> Nor where the pearl of Tethys grows:
> Much nearer and much softer glows
> The only wealth that I adore,
> And here I pay my duty:
> Our best delight
> By day or night
> Is woman's love, and woman's beauty."

Suddenly there was a disturbance at the lower end of the hall. A gray-haired baron strode forward crying, "Treason! Treason!" And after him came a knot of human men-at-arms, dragging a prisoner between them.

At once the whole hall was silenced.

"What is this treason?" said the Count mildly.

"Sire, this minstrel's ballad—" began the baron.

Cleito lost the rest of his speech, because she saw, to her horror, that the minstrel captive was Will the Wanderer.

Will was dressed more neatly than on All Fools Day— else he could not have gained admittance to this feast. He wore sandals and a green-and-white quartered minstrel's costume, and his brown hair was trimly cut. Otherwise he was the same dear Will. He looked at the Count now, quite undisturbed.

"Well, fellow," said the Count, after listening to the baron's stammerings, "suppose you sing us this scurrilous ballad, and let us judge of your wit."

The men-at-arms gave him room. Will strummed his lute, and sang, in a fine clear tenor which carried to every corner of the hall:

> "Thirteen times three—
> May it right lucky be,
> May it thrice lucky prove:
> Lucky for Westron
> And lucky for me
> And lucky the lass the true Count will love."

And Will, finishing his song, smiled and bowed to Cleito. Tears rose to her eyes. In this hall of cruel princes, her heart went out to the young country minstrel, a captive like herself.

Will turned to Count Horold, and said, quite like a courtier: "Well, Sire, what treason's in that? Have I not wished you luck of your new fair maid?"

The Count said: "This is a rougher song than the last. Yet it might pass, it might pass—in the right mouth! If you had been a Court bard, we might have had you whipped for impudence, and yet rewarded you after with an iron piece for a fair wit. But you they call Will the Wanderer—you are not entirely unknown to us by reputation. Fool, you are likely to prove a false prophet. That you couple lucky and unlucky numbers so is bad enough—but that you include my countesses in your knavish calculations! That will not pass in a common subject-knave. This night will *not* prove lucky for you, Will Wanderer. Guards! Take him away."

"Where, Sire?" stammered their leader, the old baron.

The Count laughed. "I see my lord Ambrose still in presence. He will have his green-cowled escort outside, no doubt. Take him to them, Hugo."

And then Cleito fainted.

When she came to herself she was lying on the bed in her cell, and Narses and Melissa were bending over her. Narses had been bathing her face with water; now he said urgently:

"My lady, you gave us all a great fright, and the Count was vexed. Now he is expecting you in his great bedchamber—we have orders to take you there as soon as you are sufficiently recovered."

"What did they do with him?" she said, beginning to tremble.

"With the Count? I have told you—"

"With the minstrel," cried Cleito. She was cold, partly because she was naked—they had stripped off her dinner robe.

"He has been sent to the Agency," said Narses sorrowfully. "There is only one punishment for treason."

"I see," said Cleito stonily.

She let them dress her now in all her harlot's finery—the sarong, the sari, the over-robe. She had no brooch now, no sharp-pointed jewels at all which might do harm to her master. She said no word as they put her into her litter, and carried her in pseudo-bridal triumph toward the great bedchamber, past the human sentinels and the fauns in horned caps. Only at the great black wooden doorway, she leaned out of her litter and threw her arms around Melissa.

"Oh, Melly," she cried, "Goddess bless you, little one, for all you've been to me! Blessed be!"

"Why, we shall not be parting for all that long, I hope," said Melissa, raising her blue eyebrows. "Even the greatest lover tires by daybreak, I think."

"Of course," said Cleito. One thing she now knew: for all their mental powers, fauns and faun girls could not read *human* minds. It was better that Melly should not, either. This way, she could not be implicated.

Goddess, whispered Cleito as they carried her in, forgive me. I can't. There will be others, surely, who will do your work. In my next life, if I have a next life, let me be a faun-girl—or a girl like Alis, who does not mind . . . .

The Count, in his nightgown, was sitting up in the great bed. Now the bearers had brought her on the litter to the bedside. It was her duty first to stand up, then go through her performance, then crawl into the bed and surrender her body to her master's pleasure.

"How beautiful," murmured the Count, sipping from a wine cup as she stood up. "Ah . . ." He put the cup down on his bedside table.

With one sweep of her hand Cleito flung off her over-robe. Next with another single movement she dashed off her sari, and in the next second had stripped off her sarong too, ripping the material.

"Well, I am here," she said, stepping naked onto the bed.

"What fury!" laughed the Count. "Well, that's an original variation! Indeed, that slow nonsense is superfluous between us. You were right to guess I'd be impatient."

He rose casting off his nightgown, and came to meet her. He gripped her white shoulders, and flung her down on the soft sheets. Then he fell upon her.

Cleito struck out as hard as she could with her open palm. The blow caught the Count full in the face, and wrenched his neck.

For fully ten seconds he lay as though stunned, his legs across her body, his hand feeling his jaw. The faun lackeys and Narses were caught in a huddle by the doorway: they had not had time to withdraw, and at Cleito's blow they had stopped dead still, as though petrified.

"That," said the Count through the silence, "is a flaying offense."

"I know," said Cleito.

Chapter
FOUR

———◆———

The Count drew back, then laughed shortly.

"Well, since there is no remedy now," he said, "before I deliver you to the torturers, my fair maid, you shall make *me* sport at least. If you mean to play rough, why so can I."

As his hands clawed at her breasts, Cleito jerked her knee up with all her force—and hit the Count exactly where she had hoped.

Horold's scream brought all the fauns running.

"Guards—guards!" he choked. "Not you, animals—bring *men*. An Agency doctor!" He rolled to the bottom of the great bed, hugging himself.

Now the men-at-arms were pouring into the bedchamber. They carried off the Count in Cleito's litter. Cleito herself they seized, and though she made no resistance they bound her wrists with a piece of rope between her steel bracelets. Then they dragged her, still naked, down two flights of steps, and bundled her into a dungeon. Here she was laid on a wooden rack, and her wrists and ankles were tied, wide apart, to the framework. Men stood by with metal instruments in their hands. She recognized the Lord Basil. There was also the First Chamberlain Nemon. He said:

"Wait, wait. You cannot do anything to her without the Count's express command."

"If you want to know why I did it," said Cleito, "I'll tell you straight away. I—"

"Be silent," said Nemon. "We are not even authorized to hear your confession."

Basil stirred impatiently. "You carry your negative authority highly, faun" he said. "I have some skill in these matters—"

"Your warrant does not extend to Ladies of the Household, my lord," said Nemon clamly. "Let be. We shall wait."

At last the Count was carried in on a litter, and this was placed on a table nearby so that he could look down on the proceedings. There was a green-robed man beside him: Cleito recognized Ambrose. The Agent had apparently been attending in person to the Count's injury; they seemed to have made up their quarrel.

"Well, begin," said the Count hoarsely. "But do not spoil her skin: she is beautiful enough to keep for afterward, even though she is a she-demon."

"Sire, she is ready to confess," said Nemon.

"Speak," said the Count.

"It's quite simple," said Cleito. "I was in love with that boy, that minstrel you condemned tonight, Count Horold. Since he is to die, I have no wish to live."

The Count snorted. "You are mad. Or lying. That is an explanation which strikes me as *too* simple. There is usually a political angle."

"There is *always* a political angle," said Lord Basil.

"Yes, well . . ." said the Count. "Apply the torture."

In a short time Cleito was screaming—she thought it best to behave naturally and not resist the impulses of her body in this respect. The men pushed heated needles under the nails of her hands and feet until she nearly fainted again.

"All right," said the Count, raising his hand. "Now, have you anything to add, girl? Remember, they will continue till you have told the whole truth."

Cleito laughed. "Do you think I would prefer Ambrose to begin flaying me? You are a fool as well as a villain, Count Horold."

"You shall pay for that speech," said the Count. "Ambrose—make sure you give her no sleepy drugs first, when you operate."

Ambrose bowed. "It shall be so, my lord Count."

"For the last time," said the Count, "will you tell us the whole truth?"

"The whole truth is that I hated you from the first moment I saw you," said Cleito. "I was in love with that minstrel as I said, and I hated my own family because they kept me from him. They're not my own family either, they hate me as much as I hate them, and they would much rather have sold you their own daughter—they've always treated her much better than me. I was nothing more than their servant—little better than a faun to them—ask any of our neighbors if you don't believe me. As for you, Count Horold, I detest all your cruelties, and I hate you above all for killing my love Will. Now, I defy you. I will say nothing more."

Ambrose said: "If I may make so bold Your Highness, this has the ring of truth. A political motive could not make the girl behave as she did. She would have given you her body first with her best art, and then have tried to harm you after, by treachery."

The Count nodded slowly. "Yes, that is so. Very well, you young whore: let us hear you sing once again, and then I shall have something to add if you have not."

The second torture was even more horrible than the first. Cleito fainted briefly before they stopped. She came to herself when they threw cold water over her face. There was blood on her body, which they now washed off. Well, she had not been raped; but whether she could still be called a virgin was a technical question of some difficulty. And it did not matter.

"Still silent?" said the Count. "Well, take this with you into hell, then. I had not decided to kill your boy friend before you struck me. I was only for giving him a fright and a whipping, after all. Now he shall suffer with you, and with equally great pain. Ambrose: can you arrange that they are operated upon in the same place? And with eyes uncovered?"

"Very easily, my Lord," said the Chief Agent.

"Why should we not be present ourselves?" said Basil. "For maximum satisfaction, Your Highness—"

"That is not possible," said Ambrose quickly. "It is strictly forbidden by the procedures of the Agency—and for good reason. Our magic is dangerous, and the presence of the uninitiated would introduce uncontrolled factors, most likely ruin the skins and spell danger also for the onlookers. No, Your Highness, I value your safety too highly—"

"Very well, very well," growled the Count. "Get on with it, then. Take her away."

They had covered her face and body with dark cloths, and she was carried, securely bound on a litter, for quite a long way. From occasional sounds, Cleito guessed at certain back streets of the city. And then an opening gate, and after that a tomblike silence.

At last she was laid down, and they were unwrapping her.

Her eyes met the gleam of a little moon haloed in the perpetual clouds: they were in a dark courtyard, open to the sky. There was a flagstoned path around the courtyard, and some large complicated object in the middle, perhaps a fountain. But she could hear no sound of water; only a strange faint humming. In other circumstances, it would have been soothing.

Now they had unbound her, and they were helping her to her feet: a couple of strong men in loose garments which she guessed were Agency robes. She could not stand alone—her bare feet still hurt badly—and the men were supporting her. Almost gently: they did not feel like torturers. Well they were not; they were *surgeons*, who would presently take her apart, and stuff her skin most expertly for the Count's delectation.

Now lights appeared, lights like violet stars springing into life upon the courtyard walls. The scene was dimly revealed. The Thing in the center of the courtyard was not a fountain, but some kind of growth—an enormous, fantastic plant, apparently purplish, if colors were to be trusted in this light. There was a huge central flower, almost a sphere like a tulip bowl two meters across, and outer petals the size of rowboats radiating from this sphere like the arms of a cross. Between the boat-petals were huge masses of dark leaves, and long stems like writhing tentacles as thick as a man's thigh. The whole Plant was emitting a strange sweet scent now; the humming seemed to be coming from it, too.

THE WILDINGS OF WESTRON

But Cleito had hardly the time to examine the Plant properly. The courtyard was fairly thronged with men in the robes of the Agency. They had their cowls up so that she could hardly see their faces. They were chanting a spell or a prayer, facing inward toward the Plant. And now another robed man appeared on the path from behind the Plant, leading a man who was naked.

At once Cleito recognized the victim.

"Oh Will," she cried, angonized. "Do you know me? Cleito Dixon. Will, forgive me—forgive me for causing your death!"

"Hello, Cleito!" said Will cheerfully. "There is nothing to forgive—you have not caused my death. For one thing the Count was lying, of course, to give you more pain— pain in your soul as well as your body. That was like him. He had certainly decided already that I should die."

"Will," said Cleito, "I pray the goddess that if we are reborn, we will be together. I—I told the Count tonight that I loved you. I was not lying."

Will was starting to speak, but his companion checked him.

"No more words," said the voice of Ambrose. "It will take more time in your case, and you have none to lose."

"Cleito, I love you too," called Will. "Don't be afraid—they won't hurt you. I'll see you after."

Cleito managed not to scream as the strong hands took hold of her. Others were pushing Will along, too. The robed men led them to two of the boat-shaped enormous petals, lying at right angles around the circuit of the Plant, and lifted them inside.

Cleito could not see Will any more. Around her rose strange huge fleshy barriers emitting a bittersweet smell. They were more like walls than petals. She did not understand. What, were they going to take her apart in *this*?

But the men were standing away. And now suddenly the gleam of the moon was eclipsed, and the violet lights were disappearing too. The sides of the boat-petal were growing upward at fantastic speed, rearing over her, enclosing her above as with a vault. She tried dazedly to struggle up the curving walls, but though she was not bound, she now found that she could no longer move at all. She was paralyzed: she could not even see any more. She could feel, though, still: and she realized that there was liquid lapping upward over her body. It stung.

She seemed to be lying on her back on the bottom of the petal. The liquid had nearly covered her body. It stung worse, deeply, intimately.

So: that was it, she thought. Not knives—the Agency men had a subtler method. Acid of the strange Plant. She would be taken apart very gently, daintily, as if by cooking, her skin floated off like crackling, her fat dissolved under it. Perhaps there would not even be pain as she died. . . .

. . . No, there would not be: Will was right. She could feel very little now, all outer sensation was going, she was drifting into a sleep. She thought drowsily, the Agency is deceiving the Count—this is not torture at all. An easeful easing easy death. At the moment of going they told you in coven-school, you had to concentrate if you had some particular wish about rebirth. If they had tortured her, that might have been easier . . . .

Her last thought, as she drifted into that final sleep, was simply Will . . . Will . . .

Chapter
FIVE

... And after death there were dreams, even as one was taught in coven-school.

She was certainly dead now, and in a more subtle body—perhaps the astral one. There was less of it: she sensed that it bulked little more than a half, certainly not more than two-thirds of her previous corporeal form. And it was different: she *knew* it was different. How did she know? She still could not see—and this was strange: sight should be clear on this plane. Ah, sight was returning: there was a gray light ahead. No gravity, only a gentle, oscillating pressure on her back.

Suddenly there was a jar. Gravity returned—under her shoulderblades, her spine, her hips. She was lying on her back in this new world. But it was a soft world, spongy. The light ahead—no, overhead—it was growing. There was enough to make out color.

Her world was a hollow sphere two or three times as big as her body, and it was colored a pale violet—if that was the right name; it looked not so much violet as a color entirely unknown to humans. Well, that was to be expected. And her body—she could see it now, and it was green. Yes, green—or pseudo-green.

She looked downward. In this life, she was still a female—of some kind. Her pubic hair was blue; feeling it now with her fingers, it seemed coarser hair than she could remember.

Her fingers were green, long, tapering to pink nails. There were only four of them, including the slender thumb. For that matter, why should there be more? It was hard to imagine a hand with more than four fingers . . . .

She had only four toes, of course, and her feet were delightfully long. She rubbed the sole of one foot upon the instep of the other—and stopped at once. Her green instep was soft-skinned, but the underparts of her feet, under her toes and just behind them, were very thick and tough. She knew instinctively that they would be marvelous to stand on, to run on . . . .

She lay there happily contemplating her new body with childish delight, running her slim fingers over herself.

She had small breasts—green ones, of course; she seemed to be green all over. A green belly, with a vertical bluish line like a seam below the navel. Passing her fingers upward over her face, she felt a little snub nose pointed ears, a thick mass of hair. Coarse hair. It was long enough to look at—it was blue. Of course—the perfect color for hair. It should be blue, just as skin should be green.

There was perhaps a name for what she now was, but she seemed to have forgotten it. She had forgotten a good deal. Not that that mattered. Just living—that was *nice!*

She laughed. And then she felt that there was something strange about her throat, the back of her mouth. When you pushed your tongue back there, there was a curious sensation, a sort of ticklish painful pleasure . . . .

As she finished exploring the three little buds in her soft palate, the light suddenly grew much more intense. She was almost dazzled. Her world seemed to be shattering, or burning up above her, a fiery hole spreading every which way. The violet sky was all gone now, revealing a gold sky beyond, and there were faces leaning in from this beyond, into her own world.

They were a bit like her, she thought, but *big*. They had brownish-white faces with very fine black hair above, and small rounded brownish-white ears. Their bodies seemed to be draped in a long flowing green skin—but not the same green as her own skin, and ending sharply at the neck, where their inner brown skin was revealed.

They were very very strong; they were pulling her out, up through the hole in the sky, into their own golden world. She cried out—a weak, half-choking cry. Then the world spun; she was standing on her toes, looking back into a dark purple hollow. At one end of this hollow lay a strange long twisted shape. It seemed to have a face, and black hair, and straggly whitish limbs. It was something like the beings that were holding her—the ghost or wraith of one. And the other ones were carefully raising it now, on strange long implements. It was not a ghost, it was more like an empty skin. How funny, she thought, a skin without a person inside!

The strong brown ones were speaking now, but their words seemed not to be making sense that she could follow. They were urging her forward. She trembled, stumbling on her new limbs like a newborn animal. From somewhere it came into her mind that she *was* a newborn animal.

After one or two lurches, she learned the trick of standing upright alone. How nice—her feet *did* work as she instinctively felt they ought to. Those pads were for walking on, the heel part was better held off the ground, it gave a little spring to your step as you moved.

The air was delicious, cool, and the whole world was full of the most heavenly scent. She knew now where the scent came from: from the big pink-purple one in the middle, out of which she had been born. Her mother—

—And with a gasp of inner delight she realized that she also had brothers and sisters. They were not visibly present here: here there were only the big brown walkers in those green outer skins which were not exactly skins. These were not her brothers; she could not feel their minds at all. Were they even people, or just imitations of people, cast skins like that other empty one, that yet merely happened to be walking about? There was no way of telling. They were a little frightening, whith their empty black or brown eyes—but at least they were offering her no violence, merely making her go with them into one of these rocklike places.

She went into the place among the Big Ones, the Empty Ones. They led her through hollow places all surrounded with flat rock, and at last into a wider cave-place or world with holes high up letting in golden light. And here she clapped her hands with delight, for there was a brother of hers present here, no, two, a brother and a sister—green little ones like herself, with blue hair and violet eyes and nice pointed ears. The brother-one looked especially pleasing.

"Chloe," he said, "Chloe..."

What is Chloe? she thought. She had not yet learned to form words with her mouth.

—Chloe is you, your name, said the green brother, not moving his lips either now. —Little sister, you are a nymph, a she-faun, and we are fauns, your *kin*, and you are one of us....

Language came flooding into the mind and mouth of the new nymph who thus discovered that her name was Chloe. Things about her began to take on greater meaning; and she found that she could even communicate to some extent with the Big Ones, though only laboriously, by moving her lips and tongue. The Big Ones were not frightening, after all: they were good-intentioned, even at times gentle, but in a careless, uncontrolled sort of way; they were big animals that might do you harm by oversight, say by bumping into you because they were clumsy in their movements.

The Big Ones were called *humans*, her brother told her; and these ones were males, *men*. Their females were *women*, but there were none of those in this particular place. There were many places in the world. The whole world was full of kin to the fauns; men were not kin, or if they were, it was only in a very distant sense. Men had come into the world a long time ago from another world of their own—which they had lost, and could not get back to.

Chloe's heart was filled with sadness for these big ones, Men. Fancy losing your own world altogether! Your *Mother*, your *kin!*

—We must be very kind to Men, thought Chloe to the others. Poor big things! No wonder they are clumsy and lost.

—We owe them a debt of gratitude, said the male faun. It was they who taught our whole world to use *words*. Before that, we could not think or speak in this fashion—not any of us, not even the Mothers themselves. It is because of this debt—and for some other reasons—that we have been instructed by the Mothers to serve Men, even though it is painful sometimes.

—Serve them? said Chloe. I think they are serving *us*. (For now the Men had brought her a bowl of sweet-smelling purple vegetables and Golden Apples. She was hungry, and began eating. The food, her first food in this life, was utterly delicious.)

—You will understand *serving* better soon, said the girl-faun. We fauns are *servants*, the Men are our *masters*. My master has asked me to explain to you, Chloe, that for your own safety you are to be sent away from here, to a house where you too will be trained as a servant.

When she had eaten her fill, Chloe was separated from the other fauns. A green-robed man with white hair took her into a small cell-like room and gave her a dull-red cloth to put around her waist. Then he looked at her for a moment, and said:

"How do you feel—Chloe? Are you well? Not tired?"

"Tired? No, Master," said Chloe. She had learned from the others that this was the proper way always to address a Man. "How should I be tired when I am but a few hours old!"

"Do you think you could walk a journey?" said the man. "Say, an hour through the country?"

She laughed, and flexed her light heels. "I think I could walk forever, Master; nay, and I can run, too." She scampered across the room to prove it, but was soon brought up short by the walls.

The man looked rather sad. "Dear child," he said, "do you remember nothing then, as yet?"

Chloe felt bewildered. "Remember? What is there to remember? I was made by the Mother this morning, so there is very little *for* me to remember, sir Master."

"Well," said the man, "I see it will take some time. This was a strong, rough Mother that altered you, and being your first time through, the effect is more obliterating . . . . Never mind that. But Chloe, now listen. Sometime during the next few days—maybe in the next few hours—you are going to start remembering *another life*. When that happens, try not to be afraid. You will not be going crazy or falling apart inside. Your *other life* will just be waking up, that's all. Will you remember this, Chloe?"

"Yes, sir Master. But I do not know what is 'another life.' Surely, all life is one. Or is it that you Men are another life?"

"Something like that. Now look, Chloe, in the past we might have kept you here longer, but as it happens there are dangers now, and they are getting worse. You must not stay in this place another hour. I am going to hand you over to another man now, a good man who will take you as his servant for a while—I hope only for a day or two. Then I think another faun will come—one who was a special brother to you, since he was in that Mother at the same time when you were there."

"Oh, my *twin*," said Chloe as a new word came welling up in her mind. "How nice! Where is he?"

The man smiled. "He's not really your twin—but I won't go into that. He's very tired, he can't move yet—the change was worse for him than for you. I don't think you should wait for him here. Come now, I will take you to your new master."

Chloe trotted obediently after the white-haired man, and shortly she found herself in a large room with wide windows letting in plenty of golden light. There were a number of men about, some in green robes, others in smocks or doublets. There were boxes and bundles in this place, too, and everyone seemed very busy about incomprehensible matters. There were also fauns moving in and out of a large doorway through which the light streamed in; these fauns were mostly carrying burdens.

The white-haired man took Chloe aside behind a pile of boxes, and there she was introduced to a black-haired man in a brown doublet and stout leather boots.

"Master Mack," said the white-haired man, "this is the little she-faun I was telling you of. We find she is too childish for the grave service we require in this place, but you may well make something of her. She was in any case only given us yesterday by the Chief Witch." He added, in a half whisper: "As all the relevant records already show."

"Fine, fine," said the black-haired man cheerfully. "Chloe, is it? Come along, Chloe."

Chloe hastily said goodbye to the white-haired man and

followed Master Mack out through the doorway. She found herself under the sky again, and was almost dazzled by the light.

Behind her reared a great building in dark stone, and on the left lay a sheet of blue-gray water with big white things standing up from it and moving slowly over it. In front of her was a muddy road, and beyond that, greenness. Another word came up from nowhere into Chloe's mind this was the *country*. And then a whole thinking: *you are out of the city, Chloe*. She knew that it was her brothers and sisters thinking for her. She thought back at them: *Thank you*.

Master Mack beckoned to her, and she followed him along the road to the right. *To the west*, came the thought.

Chloe was almost too happy to attend to the friendly inner voices. The world was even more beautiful than she had imagined. On their right, the walls of the dark building gave way to the lower yellow stone walls of the city; above these, the whole top half of the world was white and gold *clouds*. Then on the left there were green *fields*, the same color as her skin, with every so often black, brown or yellowish long things sticking up and ending in another mass of green or sometimes of purple—*trees*. The trees with the purple leaves—those were *kin*: you could eat of their fruits. The green ones, even though they were the color of your skin, you couldn't eat anything of them, they might even be bad for you, they were *not kin*.

How strange; thought Chloe, facing the first intellectual puzzle of her new life: shouldn't my skin be purple, if I am kin to the purple trees?

Suddenly the world seemed to spin about her, and for a few moments the scene lost its bright colors, and became a vague haze. A thinking happened deep, deep in her brain, and it did not seem like the voices of faun friends. *I am a human girl*, came the thought, *Cleito: what am I doing here, dressed in this small green shape?*

Master Mack was holding her by the shoulders and speaking to her. The spasm passed; the world brightened again and came into focus.

"Are you all right, little one?" repeated the man.

Chloe laughed. "Yes, I'm all right, Master: I must have

been dreaming, I think, not looking where I was going. I will pay more attention now."

Mack looked at her curiously. "I see you're definitely one of *those*," he muttered. "You don't speak quaint enough to be quite ordinary, and there's something about your eyes ..."

"What is wrong with my eyes?" said Chloe anxiously.

"Nothing *wrong*, but they're an unusual color for a faun. More like dark-blue than violet. Very pretty actually. But I'll show you when we get to my house. Come on, now."

Chloe began to wonder about the color of her eyes, and also how Master Mack could show them to her. How could you *see* what you saw *with*? But as she puzzled over this, the spinning started to come on again, and a voice whispering in that heart-turning fashion "... *Cleito* ..." Hastily, she stopped thinking altogether. She concentrated on the road before her feet, and on her feet moving over it, and the odd sensations stopped.

Her slim long feet were beautiful, pressing down on the slightly sticky mud. She could walk easily as fast as Master Mack—in fact, she had to go slowly so as not to pass him and leave him behind. It was pretty, the way her steps kicked up the hem of her red cloth with every stride. Maybe that was why she had been given the cloth—for an ornament in walking. She didn't need it to keep warm; the world was quite warm enough for a faun girl in her bare skin—naturally, since the world was also a sort of mother, a great kin-thing, and about half the creatures in it were kin, too.

Only half: she was becoming able to distinguish which ones. Blue grass and purple trees, yes; green grass and trees, no. Some flowers yes, some no: the kin ones had blue or purple stems. There were two sorts of birds: the kin birds had six limbs, with a pair of small four-fingered hands in front of their wings. Similarly the beasts in the fields: the ones with only four limbs, the ones that ate the green grass, these were kin to men, not to fauns; they also had lost their world, poor things, when the men had brought them here. The kin beasts, such as those hexips in that blue meadow, all had six limbs.

Then why don't I? thought Chloe suddenly. Why have I only *four* limbs, unlike all the other kin beasts?

An answer came welling up, without any uneasy sensations: *We fauns also had six limbs once. In the beginning, we had wings: we could fly....*

Fly? thought Chloe. Oh, how sad to have lost *that!* To fly like a sphinx, like a bird!

But now, came the inner voice, *we can run better than any bird; and we are big enough to think and speak.*

Chloe cheered up. Perhaps after all it was better to be a faun and admire the birds from below. If you *were* a bird, you couldn't exactly admire yourself, could you? She reached out with her mind to a little handibird sitting on a tetron tree, and entered into the bird's feelings. No, he did not rise to admiration: there was great joy and great fear—but nothing that could be called *thought*.

They were passing other travelers now—men and women on hexips, with faun servants trotting by their sides. Chloe mentally greeted every faun as they passed. It was easy and pleasant; they were all her brothers and sisters. The only *strangers* about were the humans, and some of these were very strange indeed. One man rode by all encased in hard gleaming stuff, even his head, so that it wasn't easy to be sure there was a man inside at all. Mack drew her aside to stand still and quiet while this one passed. As for the others, every one of them was thoroughly muffled up in cloths, hiding the breast, so that she wasn't sure which were males and which were females unless she picked up the truth from their faun servants. These humans even covered their *feet,* as though they were afraid to make contact with the surface of the world. Well, it was not *their* world, really—could it be bad for them to touch it, like eating the non-kin food? No, that couldn't be so for here was a little human child playing in front of a small house, and he was barefoot. Chloe drew abreast of Master Mack and looked at *his* feet: his boots had soles twice as thick as her thumb. She asked him, *why?*

Mack smiled. "Most of us don't like to get our feet muddy. Anyway, we need stout shoes, all except the lightest or hardiest of us, when we go traveling. It's the gravity. We weren't designed to walk in so much weight. I wish we were as light on our feet as you fauns."

They turned off the road by the city wall now, and struck out into the country by a narrow track between purple hedgerows, until they came to a large village.

"Crossways," said Mack. "My place!"

It was a fairly bustling place clustering around an intersection of main roads, but Mack led Chloe to a house in a side street. He paused outside.

"Chloe," he said seriously, "if any man should question you, I want you to tell him this story. It is important that you get it right! Listen: you used to belong to the Chief Witch. Repeat that!"

"I used to belong to the Chief Witch," said Chloe blankly.

"Yesterday she sold you to the Chief Agent."

"Yesterday she sold me to the Chief Agent."

"And today the Chief Agent sold you to Master John Mack."

"And today the Chief Agent sold me to Master John Mack. Master Mack, please," added Chloe, "what does 'sold' mean?"

"We can go into that later," said Mack. "Come on in now."

In the course of the next few hours, Chloe learned a great many things. She discovered that Master Mack was a *merchant*, that he kept giving people things and getting other things from them. A lot of these things seemed to be rings of *iron*, all the same size. Iron was a heavy stuff, rather rare in this world, and therefore people were very fond of it. They even handed over fauns and faun-girls to each other in exchange for this stuff, and Master Mack did this too—that is, he was a *stock dealer*. At the moment, Chloe was supposed to be part of his *stock*. There were several other fauns in the house, waiting to be exchanged in this manner. One was a faun-girl with two little twin babies. Chloe was fascinated by this family, and soon forgot about iron rings.

There were other humans in the house, too: a grown-up female and her two children, a boy and a girl. For some odd reason, Master Mack called these "my wife" and "my children"—apparently they had been living in this house with him for a long time. They seemed kindly folk, and Chloe liked the children especially. They were half-grown ones, about the size of adult fauns, and amusing with their comic, pleasantly ugly faces, their golden-brown skins, pointed noses and rounded ears.

And quickly now, Chloe found out the meaning of *being a servant*. It meant that you always had to do what the humans told you to do, even if the thing seemed dull or silly. A lot of this entailed pushing or pulling things, or carrying them, and some of this was really hard work. Carrying a pitcher of water on your head, for instance—it was almost hurtful on your neck! But the other fauns told her that she had to do it.

"The Mothers have told our people to obey the humans in everything," they repeated.

Well, that was that—it was what the fauns in the dark building had said, too. The Mothers had made the faun-folk in the beginning, and some of them could speak, and their orders had to be obeyed, and so the humans' orders had to be obeyed as well.

" 'Tis not always of the easiest," said the girl-faun with the babies to Chloe, with a touch of sadness. "Master Mack and his family are gentle humans, but my last master was not. I am right glad he sold me. I wonder, what will my next be like?"

Thus it dawned on Chloe for the first time that some men were—the word was *bad*. They would try to hurt you, and you could not easily stop them, except by running away.

" 'Tis because they are unhappy, in truth, I think," said the she-faun. "But that helps not *us*."

Master Mack added confirmation: he too was obviously frightened of certain other men. He said something about "the Count."

"I do not understand," said Chloe fearfully.

"Good," said Mack. "The less you understand, at present, the better for all of us, Chloe. If anything should go wrong, you will be taken as simpleminded, even for a faun. Now, repeat your *story*."

"I used to belong ..." When she had finished, Chloe said, "Master Mack, now can you show me my eyes?"

He led her into a room where there was a bed and a table and a gleaming thing on the wall. In the middle of the gleam, Chloe suddenly saw moving shapes. One looked like a twin of Master Mack. The other was a faun-girl in a red sarong-cloth. The gleam-shapes imitated every gesture that Mack and Chloe made. Then Mack explained.

Chloe stared. "You mean that *is* me?"

"Yes. It is how you look to me, for instance."

Chloe peered intently. Then she drew in her breath. "Yes—the eyes—they are darker than the other girls'! Than any other faun-girl's I have ever seen! Why is that?"

"If *you* don't know," said Mack uneasily, "then I'm sure I don't want to. Chloe, now will you run along to my wife? She would like to show you how to wait at table. All this is just so you know how to behave, while you're with us. We want you to pass as an ordinary faun-girl."

Waiting at table, Chloe found, was rather fun. The things to be carried in were not so heavy, and it was interesting to see how and what the humans ate. Mostly, though, their food smelled rather nasty, especially the things which seemed to be *pieces of dead animals*.

Afterward, she ate her own lunch with the other faun servants—sweet-tasting parakale and faun-bread and nuts and Golden Apples. She asked the others why humans ate such horrible food.

An old male faun shrugged. "Who knows why they do anything? I'faith, they are all a little touched i' the wits. They do not *have* to eat other beasts. But humankind seem to enjoy killing things. Mayhap they kill the *sheep* and the *chickens* for sport, and then wish not to waste the body substance. I have seen even small human children throw stones at quite harmless birds; a sheep or a barnyard fowl is not so easy to miss."

By the evening, Chloe had lost her first innocent delight in the world. Already she was aware of fear, indeed of horror; and all of that centered on humans. Even the "good" humans, like those in this house, now seemed to her faintly disgusting. Perhaps because of their carrion diet, from close to they did not even *smell* very nice. She began to think idly how nice it would be if she could run away to a place where there were *no* humans.

She was thinking this especially strongly as she was

helping to serve the meat course at dinner. It was already sunset, and the candles had been lighted. And then suddenly there came an uproar from the front of the house. The noise came again: heavy blows on the front door, and shouts of men.

Mack sprang up from his seat at the head of the table. "Out by the back!" he cried to the woman and her children.

The humans were rushing from the room. Mack, shepherding them out, turned for a moment to Chloe.

"You—follow," he said. The other faun servants he ignored.

Chloe ran after the humans. But as they crowded toward the back door, strange men came bursting into the house from that direction. They wore leather jerkins and helmets and boots, and carried blockwood maces; their leader was an elderly man with grayish hair and a grayish-brown face, dressed in a suit of metal rings.

"Stand—stand in the Count's name!" he shouted.

Chloe was sure at once that she did not like these people. She could see that the Mack humans were terrified of them. The men with the maces were waving their rods of wood as though they would like to hit people with them—even Mistress Mack and her shrinking children.

The Mack humans made no resistance. The children, huddled against their mother, were crying. And now the strange men were putting ropes around Master Mack's wrists.

PART II:

Turn of the Wheel

Chapter
SIX

Chloe was pushed into a chamber where she found all the other fauns of the house herded together, squatting on the floor. A couple of men in leather were guarding them, leaning in the doorway, scowling.

"We won't get anything out of this lot," growled one. "You never do."

The other grunted. "Sword dammit, why couldn't Basil put us on to questioning the *people?* That merchant's wife looks as though she might be fun to persuade."

"Watch your language," said the first man, nodding at the fauns. "The stock might repeat it where you wouldn't like. *Lord* Basil is touchy."

Now the gray-faced man in the rings came in, and the leather-men straightened up and slapped their maces as though this meant something. The man in the rings was holding a piece of paper.

"All right," he said, bustling forward. "I have the stock list. Now let's begin."

Chloe watched, frightened, as the men took the fauns one by one and fired questions at them, the gray-faced man looking from time to time at his piece of paper. The other men twirled their maces threateningly, but found no excuse to use them; everything the fauns said about themselves seemed satisfactory. And they knew very little about Mack and his family, for none of them were permanent servants. All were kept only for a time, and then sold to other masters. As each faun passed the tests, he or she was bundled out of the room.

Chloe was last.

"Aha, Sir Hugo," said one of the leather-men, winking. "Here is a pretty little thing for you! Young, too."

Sir Hugo was the man in the suit-of-rings. His grayish face brightened when he looked at Chloe.

"How old are you, little creature?" he said.

Chloe stared for a moment; then a phrase came up in her mind: *fourteen years*. "Fourteen years, I think, Master."

"The nicest age for a nymph," said Hugo, licking his lips. "Why, little faun, where did you get your eyes?"

"From my Mother," said Chloe promptly. And then a voice said inside her: NO WORD MORE ABOUT THE MOTHERS!

"Great Sword!" laughed Hugo. "A witty answer—but you must not be pert with me, Chloe. What has happened to your twin?"

"I do not know. I used to belong to the Chief Witch, and then..."

After a few minutes, Hugo scratched his gray curls. "This is a funny one! You're a bit on the simple side, aren't you, Chloe? No memory of anything much before today. Well, Mack said he'd just bought a faun-girl who was too daft to serve in the Agency; that checks."

"Couldn't we try and help her memory a little, Sir Hugo?" said one of the men, waving his mace.

Hugo looked displeased. "No, no. One never gets anything useful out of fauns anyway. This is a mere formality; everything is in order. In any case, Lord Basil has enough evidence on this traitor to get him flayed. This girl merely confirms what we already knew—that Mack is an agent for the Ring Church *and* the Agency. Not exactly a crime officially, but suspicious, and one of his contacts was the Governor's envoy from Trinovant. All right, let's pack this up. You, Chloe, you come with me."

They took her to a small room with a desk and piles of paper, and here she found a man of middling age, lounging on a chair with his back to the desk. He was dressed in a red-and-black doublet and leather boots. He had a hard mouth, intent black eyes, and a long scar down one cheek. He frightened Chloe more than any man she had ever seen—an inexplicable horror seemed to stir in her

THE WILDINGS OF WESTRON 69

mind, like the memory of a nightmare. And even Sir Hugo seemed afraid of him.

"Here—here, Lord Basil," said Hugo, bowing and handing over his paper. "It all checks."

Basil was toying with the handle of something in his belt. He now half drew this, and it gleamed in the candlelight: a metal knife. Then he slapped it home in its sheath, and got up.

"Then possibly we can be moving," he said, staring at Chloe all the while. "Why have you brought this one along?"

"This is the idiot nymph Mack mentioned. She won't make anybody a very useful servant, I think, when we confiscate the stock. So I was wondering if—if you could do me a favor, my lord . . ."

Basil showed his white teeth in a frightening grin. "Don't tell your favor, Hugo, I can guess. All right, you can have her."

"She—she might be interesting to breed from," flustered Hugo. "She has these unusual eyes, and I don't mind fauns who are a bit stupid. You know I make it my hobby—"

"*Everyone* knows what you make your hobby, Hugo," said Basil with a grating laugh. "All right, and I'll do you an extra favor. You are excused duty as from now. *I'll* take the traitors and the rest of their stock to the Westgate—you can speed back with your booty to Alven, to your warm bed."

And even the common leather-men tittered.

It was an hour's journey to Alvern Manor on hexipback. The first sensation for Chloe was a strange one: when Sir Hugo placed her before him on the steed's forward waist, the thought came: *I have done this before.*

"Sidesaddle?" chuckled Hugo. He gripped her. "No, not like that. That's the way human ladies ride, Chloe, and you're no lady! Swing your little green foot over his neck—yes, like that."

They went on thus, Chloe riding astride with her sarong pushed up high on her thighs, and Hugo steadying her—even after she had quite got her balance. He had usually one hand on her bare waist or her bare thigh, and she could feel the heat of his body close behind her, and the sound of his breathing close above her head. She did not like his smell.

It was dark, but the party knew their way. At last they passed through the deserted streets of a village, clattered over a wooden bridge, and came up to an imposing blockwood gateway guarded by men on foot with a couple of paracans, the six-legged native dogs of Dextra.

"We're home," said Hugo. "This is your new home, Chloe—Alvern."

They trotted up a drive between dark trees, and then came upon a wide-spreading single-story house with lights in its windows. When they had dismounted and gone inside, Chloe was pleasantly surprised: the interior of Alvern House was beautiful. There were torches burning in brackets, revealing a big hall with corridors leading out of it. The colors were mostly black and white, the walls being of two sorts of wood, light and dark, with tubolia stems bound in clumps to form pale columns supporting the ceiling. There were also colored cloths on the walls, some woven with pictures of men, fauns and animals, others painted with a design of black torches on a white background. Words welled up in Chloe's mind: *The coat of arms of Sir Hugo Brunner.* She did not bother to question her informants: she was gazing at the many other splendors of the place. The whole house seemed much more beautiful and elegant than that of poor Master Mack.

But she had no time for sightseeing now. There were faun servants about, mostly young females, and Hugo summoned a couple of these.

"Draw a bath for Chloe here," he said. "Lucy, Lily—I want you to get her nice for tonight."

Chloe thought she was going to be left alone with these faun-girls—but no, Hugo followed too as they went through the house to a stone-flagged courtyard at the back. Here he sat himself down on a bench, while a faun lackey brought him a cup of wine, and watched Lucy and Lily making Chloe "nice."

They took off her cloth, and Lucy fetched a pitcher of water and threw it over her. Then Lily began rubbing her with a sweet-smelling ball of stuff that melted on her skin.

Hugo sauntered up and began fingering various parts of

Chloe's body. He rather interfered with the washing, and Chloe thought, How silly, I wish he'd stop that.

At last he desisted, and went back to his bench, and the faun-girls dried her and began combing her hair.

She served at table that night—for the second time. It was supper for the lords of Alvern, and Chloe was feeling quite sleepy, but she had to stand and pass plates to her new masters.

Gradually she discovered who the other humans were. A younger man than Hugo, with a white face, neatly dressed, was called Norbert; and a well-grown boy, darker-faced, was called "Hugo-junior." Norbert was old Hugo's *son*, and Hugo-junior was Norbert's *son*—whatever that implied. A "son" was a baby boy, she knew, but how could a male have a baby? Perhaps human males were different in this respect. And there was a woman, too, Norbert's *wife*. Ah yes, Mack had used that puzzling word . . .

Mate, came the thought from the other servant. *Humans keep one mate for a long time.*

How strange, thought Chloe, and looked at the faun-boys, a pair of twins who stood by a corridor entrance down the hall. She already had some vague ideas about mating. It was a thing you did when you wanted a pair of babies. The other faun-girls had told her that it was very nice. You had to go with a faun-boy for that, just for a little while. And—yes, Hugo had said he wished to breed from her. She would have to go with some faun-boy. Well, that pair down the hall looked quite handsome: either of them would do. They would *smell* nice, too; all fauns smelled nice.

Chloe by herself would not have got much impression of the Brunner family—she was too sleepy—but she couldn't help picking up the feelings of the other fauns. *The younger the worse; the wife and Norbert—bad; above all, keep away from the boy.*

This message alarmed Chloe, and roused her for a while. But the boy did not do anything frightening just then: he merely looked at her in a curious way once or twice. So she lapsed back into her semi-stupor.

At last the meal was over. Oh, I hope they'll let me

sleep now, thought Chloe. She was hungry, too, but even more tired.

Sir Hugo was summoning her. Mechanically, she obeyed.

It was not far to walk, and now they were in a well-furnished room with a large bed in it. Lucy and Lily were with them also, but Hugo made them lie on the wooden floor. Then Hugo told Chloe to lie on the bed.

It was deliciously soft.

"Oh," she said, "am I to sleep here? How kind you are, Master!"

Her eyes were closing. "Hey, not so fast!" said Hugo, shaking her. He said something to the other girls, and they took away the torches and brought a little oil lamp instead, which left the room quite dim. Now Hugo took Chloe's cloth off her; he seemed to have lost his own clothes already.

It was the first time Chloe had seen a human naked. They looked very much like fauns, apparently, and Hugo was even a bit hairy on his legs. But she was really too sleepy to care very much. And then Hugo jumped upon her.

Chloe was really astonished. What was he up to? Was he punishing her? But she had done nothing wrong, had she? No . . . and he *wasn't* punishing her, either. He was pushing his own body against hers, and trying to *kiss* her. This was grotesque, for being a human he didn't have the right sort of tongue to kiss properly—much too short. Those buds at the back of her mouth—she knew that *they* were meant for kissing, and Hugo couldn't reach those, no matter how hard he tried. Well, he had given up trying, now; *that* was a relief. His little tongue was out of her mouth, and he was squeezing her breasts instead. Not too hard to hurt, luckily . . . and now he had given up even that.

What was he trying to do now? Pushing his thing, his pinner down there, into her socket. Well, at least that didn't hurt. It was no pleasure either, but it didn't hurt. And for some reason it seemed to please *him*. He was breathing very hard . . . .

Chloe relaxed and let Hugo proceed with his strange pleasure. After a while he jerked several times, and then lay still. She was a little alarmed for him—but no, he seemed to be all right, after all. His breathing was continuing, but quietly. Presently his body unstuck itself from hers, and he rolled away.

At last, real relief! She had been very hot with his enormous weight on her, and half crushed, even on the softness of this nice bed. Now she was cooler, and she didn't have to smell Hugo so much. Better still, he was falling asleep, so perhaps now *she* could, too . . . .

As her consciousness unfocused, a voice said: *What has happened to me? The Count . . . have I obeyed the goddess after all?*

She slept.

Her dreams that night were curious: she seemed to be a human girl, and she was wearing those muffling garments, many of them, and metal things on her wrists. People were calling her *Cleito*. Then human men—one was that Lord Basil—they were dragging her down onto a thing like a bed, but hard—even in her dream it felt hard. And they were going to do horrible things to her. She screamed.

And woke. There was a gray light in the room, and a man beside her on the soft bed. He shook her crossly.

"Little bitch, what's the matter with you?" said Hugo. He yawned.

Even though she did not like him very much, Chloe clung to him.

"O Master, I had such a frightening dream—"

"Oh *no!* Have I got to worry about the *dreams* of *cattle!* You're not even much fun to fool with, even though you may be pretty to look at. Pretty idiot! Here, get away with you! Lily, let's have you in here now!"

By breakfast time, Hugo had forgiven her. When everyone was washed and fed, the lord of Alvern decided to go out on an excursion, a ride round his manor, and he took with him his favorite servants—the faun-girls Lily, Lucy and Chloe. The master trotted along on his hexip, with the nymphs all three trotting beside him.

Chloe learned that this was a common custom of his. He used his male fauns mostly as farm workers, but his personal and house servants were nearly all nymphs. Lucy explained mentally: *He thinks we are prettier than the boys.*

Chloe considered Hugo's ideas of beauty quite faulty. But at least his estate was a pleasing place. There was, at the back of the house, a wide green park with large non-kin trees: *beeches, oaks, elms, pines, cedars.* Beyond this in a wide ring came a wood of purple-leaved tetron trees, their red-brown quadruple trunks clustered firm together like artificial house pillars, with here and there, for variety, a Greater Mandrake. This tree also had four trunks, widely spread black ones which untied to form a single main body higher than the head of a mounted man. The cleared path or ride through the wood ran under these trees, between the fourfold trunks, so that as they trotted along they kept moving under the dark double arches of living wood. Chloe liked these trees. They were somehow reassuring, they reminded her of that Plant Mother . . . .

From Lucy and Lily she picked up ideas of the layout of the estate. The purple ring-wood marked the limits of the house grounds. Beyond was a fence, high but not very strong in places. One could push through, but that one *didn't* do, it would offend the Masters. Beyond? Beyond was a patch of green fields used for pasturing sheep, also part of the estate; then a small wood of mixed trees, then a small river, the Avon.

"Now, how about some sport?" said Hugo, reining in his hexip. "There, girls—*senties!*"

Chloe saw a little kin-creature darting about in the blue undergrowth. Lucy made a rush for it, and Lily followed. The little creature sped away. Chloe got a momentary glimpse of it. It was like a very small hexip, but had only four legs, the forward limbs being a pair of little arms.

Apparently the game was to catch these creatures. Laughing, Chloe joined in too, but the senties were much too quick. There were many of them in the bushes, but they always got away. Hugo came riding in with his hexip, flattening the bushes, shouting ineffectual encouragement.

Chloe turned to her lord. "Sir Master, what would you do if we did catch one?"

"Why, chop off its head, of course," said Hugo, grinning.

Chloe felt a shock of horror. "But why?"

"Sport. Hunting. You are my pack of hounds, little nymphs."

"But you could not even eat it," said Chloe.

"That's not the point," said Hugo impatiently. "Sword dammit, I don't have to argue with *you!*"

Calmly, Chloe, came the thought of the other girls. *He only wants to see us run about. When he really wants to kill senties, he comes here with kin-dogs.*

Hugo now called off the mock hunt, and they proceeded along the ride till they had circled the grounds and reached the main front gate. Here there were those men guards. They had the gate open, and were talking to a pair of—

Chloe realized with a start that she couldn't quite make out *what* these two folk were.

One looked like a faun-boy, a very handsome one with dark, brownish-purple eyes. He was naked, and shaped exactly like a faun—but Chloe could hardly feel his *mind* at all. His feelings, yes: he was nice and loving, she knew that. But his thoughts were a blank. Her own mental words, *Who are you?* raised no answer from him: it was almost as though he were a human. This she had never known before. The other—

This was even more startling; it was almost the opposite case. He looked like a man, an old man with a bald head and a short gray beard, brown-faced and wrinkled, dressed in a brown frieze jerkin and leather boots. From the details of his dress, he might almost have been a trader, like Master Mack. But his *inside*—

He was a kin creature. Of this there could be no doubt: the perception was automatic. Chloe knew that when he came to eat, he would eat parabread and kin-nuts and Golden Apples, not human food. He was like a man's skin with a faun's mind inside, and yet, not even quite that. His feeling was not *gentle* like a faun's; it was almost terrible. She had heard that there *were* some terrible kin creatures, *leos, tigroids*—but not in this part of the world, and anyway they were not very intelligent, and had six limbs. What was this terrible kin-man, then?

A powerful inner voice almost smothered her: SILENCE!

She stopped thinking, and concentrated on standing upright.

Now she heard the kin-man speaking to her master. He had a deep, mellow voice.

"Well, Sir Hugo, I do believe you have made a good bargain with me. Wender is a good boy, excellent pedigree, and quite interested in nymphs, I assure you. Only he's a little shy, almost like a human in that way. Otherwise, I think you'd have had good proof of his vigor already, what with those pretty nymphs here. Well, since you are so well known as a keen faun breeder, I thought I'd give you the first refusal, my lord."

"All right, Master Peders," said Hugo, "I know you for an honest dealer. I'll give him a trial. But three pieces is a goodly sum."

"I couldn't take less, my lord," said Peders smoothly. "He's a dark-eye, and they're almost legendary. You almost never see two together, and yet here we have just that. Of course, money back if no satisfaction."

"Humph," said Hugo, and looked round at Chloe. "Satisfaction? He may have a hard job there."

"He's especially good with young ones, if I may say so, my lord," said Peders quickly. "Tickles them up nicely, so that they are more responsive afterward—er—to all *sorts* of embraces. If you take my meaning, my lord."

Hugo laughed softly. "That'll do, trader. Well, we shall see."

They all went up to the house, but there Chloe was sent about household tasks, and she saw no more of the trader Peders; nor, for a while, of the faun-boy Wender, though she kept looking out for him.

At luncheon all the family was assembled. By now Chloe had seen something of the way Norbert's wife behaved to her nymph servants, and she was in great fear of her. Luckily, at lunch she was called upon to wait on Sir Hugo.

The family's conversation during the meal was quite boring to Chloe. It turned largely upon various numbers of pieces of iron, and on humans and places she had never heard of. When Norbert's wife and Hugo-junior left the table at the end of the meal, the other two lingered. Norbert began a story about a place called *Westron*.

"I rode down to Crossways this morning, and met certain fellows from the Palace," he said smoothly. "It is credibly reported that the Count received the ambassador of Akhor last night—a private audience."

"What! The Old Emir's man?" said Hugo, sounding surprised. "We were nearly at war with those pirates last winter."

"And may be again soon," said Norbert. "Rumor has it the *young* Emir Barak is chafing against restraint—you know he has almost an independent princedom, and a good fleet of his own. But his father is a politician, and he realizes we are not to be trifled with. Doubtless the Count has shown the ambassador that death-thrower the Sword-god has blessed him with. I don't think we need fear any raids once the ambassador has taken his tale home with him, and the old Emir has spoken to the young one." He paused. "One of my friends told me the ambassador even wants an alliance with us."

"Impossible, surely," said Hugo, raising his eyebrows. "We are Swordists, and the subject folk are of the Ring—but both our churches have the same origin, Sword-god and Ring-goddess are husband and wife, though they may have their little quarrels .... But the Akhorians are utter enemies to all our covens, they're Lordists of the worst kind, they have their Old Scriptures which say they must not suffer any one of us to live."

"Lordists—Swordists," said Norbert with a smile. "I have sometimes wondered, Father, whether they are so different, at bottom. I know our Swordist Church began in extreme hatred of the Saints, but in our very enmity over the centuries we have become more similar. If it were politic to stress the similarities, I'm sure that could be managed. It would be an excellent blow against the Governor of Trinovant ..."

At this point, Chloe stopped listening altogether. It was all meaningless words.

Norbert Brunner, the heir of Alvern, looked around for a moment at his father's new acquisition, that dark-eyed faun girl. Appalling, disgusting: the old man was making himself a byword, bringing the family into disrepute. He turned back to him.

"Father, has it ever occurred to you, since my mother's

death, that it might be more fun to interfere with *human* girls? I'm afraid Junior has caught the idea from you—and it's all so unnecessary."

Hugo flushed. "I don't want to breed any bastards, Norbert; I've always liked nymphs, too—and what of it? It's *because* they are cattle that they give me the most pleasure. Because I *own* them."

"I understand *that*," said Norbert. He sighed. "One more point in favor of the Akhorians. They have *human* cattle—they call them *slaves*, you know. If we do ally ourselves with them, it's quite on the cards, father, that we will have slaves too, soon. How would you like that? If we had slave wenches around here, instead of these animals? I'm sure they would do young Hugo good, too."

"What difference would that make to him?" grunted his father. "He only whips his nymphs, anyway."

"Not *only*," smiled Norbert. "*First*. That's all right—it's a rational pleasure—it's what comes after I object to. I don't like perversion. Now with a human slave girl, he could whip her and use her after in the manner for which Nature designed her. A great improvement."

"Norbert, you're too cruel," said Hugo, shuddering. "You're not a good Swordist."

"On the contrary, father, I'm a perfect Swordist. If I had not been your heir, I think I'd have been happy to go into the Church. Consider: our church broke away from the Ring on just these grounds. Both Ring and Sword agree that Good and Evil are mutually necessary, don't they? But quite arbitrarily, those soft Ring-folk only like Good. Our founder, First Swordsman Newton"—he bowed his head in reverence—"pointed out that Evil has its rights as well. You must be at least partly Evil to maintain the Great Balance. Evil ... cruelty ... they're certainly part of Nature, the Great Oneness. I'm not in the least ashamed of my cruelty; I cultivate it in all piety, natural piety. Nature gives no quarter to the conquered, and I don't see why we Conquerors should. Slavery, for instance, is a perfectly natural institution—it flourished everywhere in the best periods of Old Tellus." He stretched, and yawned. "Good Sword, father, do you object to cruelty, and yet follow Lord Basil?"

"I only do my duty," said Hugo weakly.

"Then you should do more," said Norbert seriously. "Father, next time Basil calls for you, please take me along. I have wanted to serve him for some time. I have a feeling that he will go far, very far."

When Chloe was not actually working, she had no particular place to be in this house. The faun-girls slept anywhere on the bare floors, in the hall, in the kitchen, in the corridors, but most often at slack times would gather in the courtyard behind the kitchen. And Chloe was here, late that afternoon, when she saw Lucy approaching from the outbuildings to the left and behind the house.

She smiled at Chloe. "Come, girl," she said. "Master's orders: ye are to meet a new friend."

Chloe's heart leapt with excitement, for she felt the meaning of Lucy's words. Her "new friend" was to be a boy-faun, and that boy would be Wender.

Sir Hugo was waiting outside the shed, but Chloe hardly listened to his pleasantries. She took his general meaning: she was to be mated.

And at once.

Chapter
SEVEN

She went into the shed, and to her relief no one else came in with her. The place was a barn, with sweet-smelling native hay, feed for hexips. At first she could not see anybody. Then a figure rose from behind a hay bale, and she recognized handsome young Wender. He was naked, as before.

He ran forward, and seized her hands, and looked deep into her eyes. His own dark brown ones were strangely beautiful.

"Cleito," he said, "Cleito, my darling . . ."

"Wender?" she said uncertainly. "Why do you call me that name? It is one I dreamed of last night, a terrible dream . . ." She shuddered, moving forward to receive the comfort of his body until she was rubbing herself gently against him. He did smell nice . . . .

"Oh no," he said, drawing back slightly. "Cleito, my dear love, don't you remember anything yet? How we were plighted lovers, in the secret court of the Agency, when you thought we were going to our death?"

Chloe whimpered and nestled against him. "Lovers?" she said uncertainly. "Yes, we *are* going to be lovers, aren't we, Wender? I wonder how much time they will give us."

He looked down at her and ruffled her thick blue hair. "Time," he said. "No, they never *have* given us time, have they? Neither your uncle, nor the Count, nor impatient Ambrose, and now perhaps not this pig Hugo—and yet we need time, Cleito—Chloe—for you to come to yourself."

She raised her eyes to his. Oh, how beautiful he was! And kind, very kind; if only he would stop talking so strangely....

"Wender—wouldn't you like to—to kiss me?" she said shyly.

Wender trembled a little. She sensed a trouble in his feelings. Well, perhaps he was even shyer than she—like that man Peders had said. She would have to help him. This must be the right thing to do....

She pressed her lips against his, and slipped her long tongue into his mouth, right over his own tongue and on to the sweet little nipples at the back. Yes, this was surely right, it was what the other faun-girls had said... and he seemed to like it! His knees had given way, they were both falling, her cloth was coming off, the hay was soft...

They were lying side by side, and now at last Wender seized her around the cheeks with his long beautiful strong green hands, and pressed his tongue into her mouth, over her own tongue...

The pleasure hit her like an explosion.

It was not like touching your own mouth-nipples; that was not the shadow of this. The joy of being reached by her brother-lover flooded her whole body, it coursed down her spine to her thighs and made her thighs open and her upper knee move over and past her lover's knees. She was gathering him into her legs' embrace, not thinking at all but letting her body do what it wanted. Wender also seemed to be past thought. He was locked into her now, his boyness in her girlness. They were rolling; now she was on top of him, now he on top of her. It made no difference which way up they were, they were in a two-person world where there was no gravity. Laughter was coursing inside her body; there was a continuous ring of laughter-pleasure from her mouth-nipples down her spine through their mingled loins and up *his* spine to his tongue—yes, she felt even his half of the circuit, because his feelings were also hers. Since he no longer thought, there was no barrier between them, they had the most perfect and most delightful kind of faun communion.

The circuit of pleasure had phases or pulses in it, when the fiery ring seemed to spin shimmering into a sphere.

These were the intensest moments, when they had rolled all their sweetness up into one ball . . . .

It seemed to go on for ever. The only change was when she drew back her head, breaking the circuit for an instant, and said, "My love, now this way . . ." and put *her* tongue between his lips.

Then the circuit was reversed: she could feel it flowing down through Wender from his mouth-nipples by his spine to his pinner, then from his pinner up through her socket, her spine, her tongue . . . .

It might have lasted very much longer, but then simultaneously they both picked up a warning from outside their little world, and Chloe perceived the words: *Time to stop, he is getting impatient* . . . .

"Oh, my love," said Chloe, half weeping (but partly for joy) as they came asunder. "My dear darling mate . . ."

Wender shook his head. "Darling, afterward, when you know—I hope you will forgive me. Chloe, darling—I will see you again. Tomorrow, certainly—and then we must make plans—"

There was a noise at the door.

"Now then, you two," came Hugo's voice, "have you done it? Have you made me a couple of little dark-eyed nymphs inside her, Wender boy?"

All that evening Chloe felt that she was living in two worlds, if not more. Outwardly, she went about her duties as a house servant as efficiently as ever. She carried in pitchers, she served plates at dinner, she stood quietly to receive her master's commands. Inwardly, she was walking hand in hand with her lover through dream places. One was a courtyard with a Plant-Mother in it, and green-robed men were standing by the Mother and against the walls, bowing to Wender and herself as they passed by. Then again she was in a hall like this one, only greater and with luminous walls, and it was filled with people, some human, some fauns, some vaguely neither, but all nice and *respectful*—yes, even the humans bowed as Wender led her to one of the thrones on the dais and took the other himself.

These daydreams startled her at times. They were only

fauns, she and her mate, how could there be humans who bowed down to *them?*

"Chloe," said her master Hugo, as he rose from the table after dinner, "when you've had a bit to eat, come along to my chamber. I'd like to see what you've learned."

Chloe did not understand this remark, but she obeyed the command.

This time Lucy and Lily were not in the bedchamber, but lying in the corridor outside.

"Master thinks ye are shy," said Lucy seriously. "Dear Chloe, he will not hurt ye in body or in feelings if ye let him have his way. 'Tis nothing to us, because they are nothing to us in that manner, nor ever can be. Leave your feelings with us this night, child, and we will comfort you."

And then Chloe understood the madness of it: that Hugo was trying to *mate* with her.

She took off her cloth at his command and lay down, and he proceeded to do just what he had done the previous night. The ridiculous pitiful imitation with the tongue; the meaningless clawing at her nerveless breasts and false nipples; the pushing in with his pinner even when there was no circuit and therefore neither pleasure nor pain down there—at least, not for *her*. Hugo seemed to be getting a bit excited, though. At one moment he reared off her slightly, and said, "Hey, couldn't you wiggle a bit—and gasp, the way the other bitches do?"

So Chloe wriggled, and tried a few experimental gasps—but she had to give that up quickly, for her gasps were in danger of becoming giggles. Luckily, her performance had given Hugo just enough satisfaction, for now he jerked in that absurd way, and it was quickly over.

Luckily, too, he had drunk a fair amount of wine at dinner, for soon afterward he was snoring, and the entertainment was over for that evening.

Chloe felt the comforting friendship of the girls outside. Reassured, she fell into a doze, then into a deep sleep . . . .

Her dream was clearer than ever before. She was in the Count's bed, and Horold, hateful Horold Harkness the torturer, the usurper—he had mastered her, made her his thirty-seventh concubine. He was pleased with her performance, and he preferred her even to Estrild, his fair-haired Nordic girl.

"Dear little Cleito," he was saying, his smiling handsome horrible face close to hers, "for this you shall be rewarded: I shall let you live, you and your Will, and you will be alive when they put you on the wall. A pair of butterflies, fluttering your wings there forever. But your chrysalis will be nice too, Cleito, and I shall enjoy that in my bed, your sweet skin, Cleito, my darling—"

"No, no, *no!*" cried Cleito, waking up.

Beside her, the Count grunted and stirred in his sleep, then sighed and fell back again.

A gray light was coming into the room. Cleito scrambled back against the head of the bed, as far as possible from the loathsome body of the Count. Her movements were light, strangely agile; but shame and horror possessed her. She looked down at herself, to see what the Count had done to her. Her throat was dry, her tongue thick in her mouth, as though there were swellings behind it.

And then she caught her breath.

There was no blood on her body, but her skin, she could now see, was greenish. Her feet were—deformed: long, thin. There was something wrong about her toes. She felt them with her fingers—and almost screamed.

She had only four fingers, and they were green!

A moment later, she became aware that this was not the Count's bedchamber, nor was that man there the Count, but an older, grizzled man.

What? she cried mentally. And then a voice came up inside her. *Chloe—I'm Chloe—*

A wave of memories washed over her. Chloe was a sort of garment, a mask she had been wearing for some days. Not everything was clear, but enough. Chloe had been a mask, but also *herself*. *She* had been that shrinking little pliable shameless nymph. Shameless ... for she had done shameless things, and shameless things had been done to her. This man—that was vile enough; but yesterday there had also been a faun-boy. That memory lingered deep in her *body*. She had been *mated* like an animal, to produce offspring for her master to sell or to keep for his own horrible perverted purpose ....

Perhaps she ought to kill herself. Death . . .

But she had already died once! Or had she? No—not a true death. If this world was not some ghastly dream—but she remembered now the journey from Westron through Crossways according to "Chloe's" memories, and they checked with the geography of Westria as she had known it in her "previous life." She was at Alvern, a place she had known by reputation before. Alvern was on the Avon, not two hours' journey upstream from her family's farm.

Her family! Did they exist in this world? And if so, had the Count . . . She shuddered. People had mentioned the Count also in this life: that man Mack—and yes, Mack had been arrested by Lord Basil, the Count's bastard brother.

It was all too horribly real, too *like* the world she had known. She had known Basil—yes, and Hugo before at that dreadful feast—and neither seemed any older. She had not been reborn—just *changed*. She was now physically a *nymph*, an animal owned by this Hugo.

Coldly, she considered the problem. If there had been no death, then what? Of course—Ambrose! He had tried some hideous experiment on her, and it had succeeded. There was no limit to the Agency's magic—they could even turn you from a human into a faun, and give your superfluous skin to the Count as proof of your death! In that case, perhaps *Will* was alive too!

The thought filled her with sudden immense joy. Oh Will, she said inwardly, if you are alive, my darling, it doesn't matter too much what has happened to me!

Just to see him somewhere, if only she could find him. In what shape would he be? There was no way of telling either what he would look like or where he might be.

And maybe he wouldn't recognize her—or want her, after what had happened. Still, she would like to help him in any way she could. Will, and her family, and her friends. There was so much evil and cruelty in the world, she should help to fight it.

She put aside all thought of suicide. That was too easy. Goddess forgive her, she had more or less done it once! Not again. Now, though: what to do? Where to begin?

Cautiously, she crawled off the bed and stood up. Hugo did not awake.

She had the use of this strange body quite perfectly: Chloe's physical experience was hers. She moved lightly across the room on her animal-like pads and nymph toes, making no sound. There was a mirror on the wall, and there was sufficient light now to see herself clearly. She stood, planted firmly on the length of her feet, toes to heels, absorbing the shock: she was a young nymph, rather like Melissa, but even prettier, with dark bluish eyes. Melissa . . . she wished she could see Melissa now.

And then in a flash a plan came to her. She would escape from here and go back to her family. *If* her family were still at Avonside—but there was an even chance they might be. They might even shelter her, believe her story. Maybe Melissa would be returned to them. Anyway, it was worth trying. If she were caught, she would simply act stupid. Her master Hugo would take her back, and beat her, but surely not injure her severely, and then she could think again what to do.

Why not try it now? It was still now bright day, and Hugo was asleep. She could get past the house servants on some excuse, and then . . .

She knew the way. And nymphs could run fast, and there was a river, just in case they used the kin-dogs to trace her. And, good Goddess! The thought of staying here a moment longer . . .

Briefly, she prayed. O Goddess, if I am now a nymph—of a race dear to you, as Myrto says—give me courage and strength, and take me into your care, you who care for all wild things, all animals, all native life . . . .

She cast one look at the loathsome body on the bed and slipped to the door. It opened softly under her hand.

The nymphs Lucy and Lily were awake in the corridor. "I'm just going to wash," she told them.

"Not like that," whispered Lucy. "You must wear your cloth, it is the custom here. Chloe! what is wrong with your thought? It is hidden."

There was no time to argue or explain. She whipped back into the room, retrieved her sarong and put it on. Hugo still slept. Then she was out again, and this time the nymph-girls did not detain her. Out through the corridors, through the kitchen, into the yard, moving nimbly but not fast enough to rouse suspicion.

It was a misty morning. Good Goddess, thanks!

Past the outbuildings ... and now in some purple bushes she discarded her cloth. It would be far better to go naked; she could run faster that way, and slip almost invisibly across green fields.

The next moment a figure rose up from behind the bushes—two figures. A naked faun-girl, and a naked human boy clutching her wrist. The boy was Hugo Junior, and his face was flushed, and in his free hand he held a whip.

'H!" he cried, catching sight of her. "The pretty new one. Come here, you!"

Cleito fled at once, and young Hugo gave chase, roaring at her to stop. He was a boy of thirteen or fourteen, and he ran fast, but Cleito, on her faun feet, ran faster. Across the park she rushed, the shapes of oaks and cedars looming vaguely out of the mist, the boy's cries becoming fainter behind her. Then she dived into the purple wood and reached the fence.

She ran along this a little way, desperation rising in her. The fence was much too high to jump, if she didn't find the weak spot soon. Ah—there was a small gap.

She pushed her way through. In the field beyond, there was a flock of sheep milling about. She ran fast and wide to pass them—and almost collided with the shepherd, a male faun of mature years.

He looked at her, astonished, a slow smile beginning on his face. She could not read his thoughts—her new consciousness had obliterated that faculty—but she immediately picked up his feelings. Pleasure—and sexual arousal.

"Master Hugo does not often give us a chance with nymphs," he said, coming toward her. "My pretty one—"

"No—no, *please*," she said tearfully. "Please, my brother, I'm on important business—in the name of the Mothers—that way—"

The old faun looked at her sadly. "Go on then," he said. "But if you come back this way, sister, remember the poor shepherd Skiptoe."

"Goddess bless you, Skiptoe," she said, and rushed past.

Minutes later, she scrambled down a bank and flung

herself into the deserted stream of the Avon. The river was already deep enough here to swim underwater, and she was soon moving gracefully downstream with powerful movements of her long feet.

Chapter
EIGHT

A short distance above Avonside farm there is a wooden bridge, for here the main road from Westron to the sea passes over the tributary. Beyond the bridge lies the village of Ringston, with its round covenstead and cluster of cottages. Below Ringston bridge the Avon makes a bend, and below this again the stream is bordered by high banks and fringing trees and bushes, so that the water is screened from the land on either side.

It was even more screened that spring morning by a heavy mist which lay thick below the bridge. Cleito rejoiced at that; she passed the bridge by swimming again underwater till she was sure the mist was shrouding the surface. Then she scrambled out through the reeds and mud of the bank and walked warily parallel with the little river toward her former home. She was recognizing every clump of trees now, and irrationally felt almost safe, like a wild animal on its own familiar territory. She was tired and a bit cold now, but almost happy.

And yet, she thought, here is where I have to be really careful. How can I find out if they're here? The fauns! That's it. At least, I can try....

Moving forward slowly, she exerted her nymph's sympathy, trying to pick up mental traces.

It did not work well. Now that she had come to herself, her human personality had somehow blotted out her former powerful telepathy. She sensed vaguely that there *was* a faun nearby, but she could not even tell what sex, let alone identify the individual. There was nothing for it but to press on. She would climb that bank there, and then strike away from the river toward the house.

She topped the bank, and the mist lifted slightly—and then she stopped dead in her tracks. For a moment, her mind could not interpret what she saw.

Downstream the river was full of boats—no, not boats, *ships*.

They were too long to be boats, though they had no masts raised. They did have long mastlike yards, but these were attached like levers far forward to a stumpy wooden upright near the bows. At the moment the yards were lowered down the center of the decks—a good device to make the ships invisible from beyond the river. The ships were being rowed very quietly by double lines of men—but most strangely, they were being rowed stern foremost, both ends of each ship being much alike, and the steersman with his long oar was now operating from the bow.

Cleito immediately guessed why. There was hardly room to turn in the stream, and for a quick getaway ... They *would* be thinking in terms of a getaway, for these men were not Westrians. They looked darker-skinned than the people of Atlantis, they had square-cut short black beards and wore green tunics, leather kilts and conical metal helmets. At the belt of many a man there glinted a costly metal sword.

Cleito stood horror-struck for only a couple of seconds. Then she bounded away from the river, running at full speed for her old home.

An outhouse was looming up, when suddenly a small green figure stood before her, a figure in a red cloth.

"Why, sister, who are ye?" said a pleasant familiar voice.

"Melissa!" cried Cleito. "Melissa!"

"Nay, you have the vantage of me, sister," said Melissa, smiling but wrinkling her blue eyebrows. "Your name I know not—nor your mind neither—"

"Melissa, I'm—a friend: I can't explain more now, there isn't time. I've come to warn everybody—there are pirates in the river! Four big shiploads at least. It must be a raid. Are the Carver family here?"

"I feel your fear—" began Melissa doubtfully.

"Oh it's true, believe me! Can't we—"

THE WILDINGS OF WESTRON 91

"Come then," said Melissa, and led her quickly into the outhouse-stable. Here there were two hexips in their stalls, and a young man moodily brushing down the coat of one of them. Cadmon!

"Master," said Melissa, "here is a faun-girl with grave tidings."

"Cadmon," cried Cleito, "there are pirates in the Avon! For Goddess' sake, if your family are here, get them away at once!"

Cadmon left the hexips and sidled around Melissa and Cleito, looking at the strange nymph with utter surprise.

"What the Hades are you?" he grunted. "That's no way to talk to a Master, you little green bitch! You crazy or something?"

"Cadmon, for Goddess' sake believe me! There's not a second to lose. Those men—I think they're Akhorians. They've come up the river in the mist—and you've heard stories of what they do! I remember Uncle Luke saying only last month . . ."

Cadmon stared at her even harder. He put his hands on his hips, the fingers of his right hand toying with a bunch of keys dangling at his belt.

"Are you a black witch?" he said, backing away. "What do you know of 'Uncle Luke'? Your eyes—they're funny, too. In Goddess' name, who *are* you?"

"I'm—I'm Cleito." said Cleito weakly; and then could have bitten her tongue, for the effect on Cadmon was catastrophic.

"No," he said, backing away. "No . . ." And the next instant he had dashed out of the stable, and Cleito heard from outside the slam of a bolt as the door shut on them. She threw herself against the door, crying, "Let me out!" But at once she heard also the clink of a key in a lock.

They were trapped. And there were footsteps outside, of a man running away.

"Are you—are you a ghost?" Melissa whispered. "No —that cannot be, for I can feel your life. Mayhap y'are a changeling."

"A changeling! Yes," said Cleito, remembering an ancient legend. "Melissa, darling, try to believe me. I am your very own friend Cleito—you remember how we parted outside the door of the Count's bedchamber. Afterward, they delivered me up to the Agency to be put to death, but the Agency men did not kill me, they changed me instead, into this shape. Two or three days now I have been a nymph, I was given to a master at Alvern—Sir Hugo—and this morning I ran away from him. I was coming here and then I saw the ships in the river—"

"Cleito," murmured Melissa, staring. "The voice is different, but the eyes, the words ... and the inside of your life is not the life of a faun."

"Do you remember," said Cleito, "that Sabbat midday when I went down to the river to wash and there was nobody else there and you came swimming to me under the water and advised me to take you as my maid to the Palace?"

Melissa threw herself into her friend's arms. "O Missy Cleito, I believe now," she said. After they had done embracing, she drew back a little, and added,"Your next life came around somewhat quickly, i'faith, Mistress! Tell me now, which is it better to be—a human, or a nymph?"

Cleito shook her head, with a little shudder. "What they do to your folk, Melly—to us, I mean—it's hateful, shameful! It must be stopped. But in itself—being a faun—that's not bad at all—"

And then Melissa screamed.

"What is it?" said Cleito, clutching her.

"O Missy, there's fear—terrible fear! In Ringston, I think. And killing. . ."

The two girls clung together. Even Cleito could feel some of it—a mental wailing of fauns. "The pirates!" she whispered. "Oh, if only they'd let us out of here!"

The only windows of the stable were too high to climb to. And the next moment they heard the tramp of feet outside.

There was a scraping of metal, and the door was flung open. Cadmon was there—but behind him were strange men in green tunics and conical helmets, carrying drawn swords. Cadmon was white and trembling.

"Come out, animals," said one of the pirates, in a strange, rough accent. "You nymphs, bring out the hexips and hold them and obey every word of ours if you wish to live."

There was nothing for it but obedience. As they were

bringing out the hexips Cleito could sense Melissa's interior cries, which might be interpreted as a distress signal to the world in general. She guessed that all the other fauns in the neighborhood would be broadcasting a similar message. Could this do any good? Could other fauns summon help? Where were the Count's forces? His navy would most likely be in harbor in Westron in this dangerous weather, and by land it was a two-hour journey from the city.

At least, now the mist was lifting.

There were half a dozen pirates about the farm, and they were assembling their loot. The most prized possessions of the Carver family were being loaded on the hexips, and now Uncle Luke and Aunt Rhoda and Alis were being driven along at swordpoint like cattle. Uncle Luke's wrists were bound, and now they were tying Cadmon's hands too. Alis was weeping against her mother's shoulder.

There were no other faun servants about. Presumably Modo and Mahu had fled.

Cleito realized that there was nothing, absolutely nothing that she could do to help her relations. She could not even try to comfort them. They would think her merely a mad animal.

The prisoners and the hexips and the two faun-girls were now driven along the path to the bridge, and over the bridge, along the road, and into Ringston.

Here the village was obviously in the hands of the invaders. Squads of pirates were busy assembling booty, and the villagers—all whom Cleito recognized—were being lined up, menaced by swordpoints, against the walls of the houses. There were only men and boys in one group, packed tightly against the front of one cottage—even little boy babies were being held by their fathers or brothers in this human herd. Another group consisted of girls and young girl children.

The older women were being forced to pile armloads of kindling against the sides of the wooden covenstead. A few fauns were helping in this work—but very few; evidently most of the fauns of Ringston had escaped.

The Carver family was now split into the conquerors' categories. Aunt Rhoda was driven off to join the women workers, Alis to huddle with the young girls; and Luke and Cadmon were pushed roughly over to the wall of the menfolk. Cleito and Melissa were added to an assemblage of booty—hexips, household goods, a small flock of sheep.

At last there was a pause; the women had finished their task to the pirates' satisfaction. The pirate who had been commanding them looked to his leader inquiringly.

The pirates' leader was a man of about thirty years, with hard black eyes. The breast of his tunic was covered with a gleaming dural plate, and his helmet was circled with a diadem that had the look of expensive steel. He turned to his lieutenant.

"Inside with them, Kherev," he said, in clear, precise tones.

"Very good, Lord Barak."

The mature women were driven into the covenstead, and the doors were locked on them. Terror was in the air; Cleito needed no telepathy to sense it. Many of the village girls were sobbing, and babies wailing. The village headman, old Farmer Wiener, called out:

"See here, good strangers, you've got a fair haul from us; why'n't you take that and leave us poor folks—"

"Kill him," said Barak.

A pirate stepped forward with drawn sword and slashed Wiener across the throat. The old man fell, blood gushing from his neck like a slaughtered animal. The pirates, who seemed a tidy-minded crew, dragged his body clear of the group of men and boy prisoners.

A deathly hush fell on the village. Barak had taken a book from one of his aides, a book with a green cover. He now opened this, glared around at his captives and in a loud voice read:

"Thus saith the Lord: so it is written:

"When the Lord hath delivered them into thy hands, thou shalt smite every male with the edge of the sword,' Deuteronomy, twenty, thirteen.

"Again it is written: 'Thou shalt not suffer a witch to live.' Exodus, twenty-two, eighteen.

"Again it is written: 'Now therefore kill every male among the little ones, and kill every woman that hath known man by lying with him.

" 'But all the women children, that have not known a

man by lying with him, keep alive for yourselves.' Numbers, thirty-one, verses seventeen and eighteen."

He shut his book with a snap. "Now, as we are faithful followers of our Lord of Hosts, we shall do even as we are commanded. The female witches are within in their place of whoredom and abomination and idolatry. Guards! Apply the fire."

As Cleito watched, helpless and horrified, she saw some pirates kindle torches. Next they put these to the high-piled kindling leaning against the walls of the covenstead. The kindling was mostly tubolia sticks and other very dry pieces of wood; there was a favorable breeze, and they flared up in a few seconds. The young girls began to scream, and some tried to burst through the line of their guards, but the men beat them back with the flats of their swords or with wooden maces.

And at once the pirates began to deal with the men and boys of Ringston. At one end of the line, the guards were merely holding them back; at the other end, they had begun to slaughter them methodically. They cut the throats of all the men and bigger boys; the babies they disposed of by smashing in their heads with their blockwood maces.

Meanwhile, the covenstead was burning fiercely, and the young girls, who could see everything, were still screaming.

Cleito was in Melissa's arms. She felt paralyzed; she could not even close her eyes. Uncle Luke and Cadmon were near the far end of the men's line. At last the pirate executioners reached them. She saw their throats slashed right across, and their bodies fall writhing onto the heap of the other slaughtered human carcasses.

Feeble cries were coming out of the smoking, flaming covenstead.

"It is finished," said Barak, handing the green-covered book back to his aide. "Let us go, in the peace of the Lord."

And then the pirates were prodding their booty animals, including the nymphs and the young human girls, down toward their ships.

Chapter
NINE

The mist had altogether dispersed by the time the Akhorian flotilla reached the mouth of the Avon, the point where the tributary fell into the broad waters of Sabrina. It was even a brilliant and beautiful late morning.

Cleito and Melissa had been put into a ship along with several human girls, including Alis. But the pirates, tidy-minded as ever, had one huddle of booty animals forward which comprised the nymphs and a couple of male fauns, and another little group of captive girls toward the stern, and the two groups were not allowed to mingle. Melissa said, anguished:

"If only Missy Alis were a nymph, we could try to comfort her inside—but this way, there is no path to reach her pain!"

Cleito was coming out of the first hideous shock of the massacre. At once, she began examining the possibilities of escape. They did not seem good: each side of the ship was occupied by rowers—who were free pirates, not galley slaves—and at the points where there were no rowers, near the bow and stern, there were armed guards. The pirate leader Barak stood on a raised deck astern, surveying his booty and his whole ship and the mouth of the Avon ahead.

"Tell me quickly, Melly," whispered Cleito. "I had better know. What happened between the Count and my— my family after I ..."

"The Count was very angry," said Melissa. "He had me whipped—but not too much, for Narses spoke up for me and assured him I had known nothing of your mind. Indeed I did not! You are a bold one. Then of course he was angry with the Carvers, and held them in the palace for a day until he had checked your story with the neighbors. Lucky for them—or was it unlucky—the neighbors guessed what to say; I think their own fauns prompted them. They assured the Count's men that you hated your family, and they hated you, and so the Count let them go after they had paid back the forty pieces plus a small fine. He threw me back at them too, saying he would not have me about his Palace for a minute longer—I think he did not want to be reminded all the time of you. And yet he has already been to the outer court of the Agency, to view your cast skin."

Cleito shuddered. "I had forgotten about that. Am I not already on his wall?"

"Nay, Mistress, 'tis not yet fit for show there; the Agent's skilled artisans have yet to work on it."

"O Goddess," said Cleito, "this world is full of horrors! And all the work of men . . ."

As she was yet speaking, she sensed a disturbance among the pirates. The lookout, close above her head, uttered a hoarse cry, and the pirate chief, Barak, came scrambling along the deck and stumbled up to the bow. The ship swung slightly, and then Cleito saw a bigger ship ahead on the waters of Sabrina—a ship with the red-and-white-striped sail of the Westrian navy. Between the Westrian and their own vessel there was a second pirate ship, apparently trying to sweep around and past the Westrian. But as Cleito watched, this other pirate ship seemed to dissolve, to fold in on itself like a collapsing house of cards. At once pirates, rowers, booty and wreckage were floating in the water, and the air was filled with the cries of the victims.

This fantastic disaster was like a disappearance in a dream—there had been almost no sound till it was complete. But Cleito's keen nymph nostrils picked up a distinct smell of charred wood.

Now the Westrian ship was looming closer. On her poop there stood a single small figure, with attendants keeping a very respectful distance. This man was holding his right hand up, as though pointing at the remaining pirate vessels. Meanwhile, there were frantic hailings, shouts from one ship to the other.

Melissa whispered: " 'Tis the Count! He has the death-weapon. If the pirates do not surrender at once, we will all be killed."

The world seemed poised in a great hush. The ships were drifting closer, and Cleito could now recognize the lonely figure on the poop, and the black tube in his hand. It seemed to be aimed almost directly at her. But Barak had signaled his surrender in time; and now the remaining pirate ships came out of Avon-mouth, and one by one tied up to trees on the bank of Sabrina, while the triumphant navy of Westria—at least a dozen galleasses—hovered close by, anchoring farther out in the stream.

Negotiations went on all day. Cleito had expected that the pirates would have to surrender unconditionally, and was wondering what this would mean for herself, for Melissa and for poor Alis Carver; but things did not go quite like that.

Late that afternoon, the pirates paraded their captives in a green meadow before the Count and his officers. Even the fauns and other booty were displayed. Cleito shook her blue hair over her eyes; she did not want to attract the least attention. Luckily, neither Lord Basil nor any of the Brunner family was there.

To her amazement, she saw that the pirate chief was seated behind a table at the Count's right hand, the place of honor in Atlantis. They were chatting quite affably. Close behind them stood Nemon, the faun First Chamberlain, and several pirate officers and knights of Westron. The Count looked slightly haggard but fairly cheerful; he was toying with a black handle protruding from a leather holster at his belt. The pirate chief seemed a little subdued, but not altogether unhappy.

"Well, Barak," the Count was saying, "I think we have taught you a useful lesson, and you will listen to your father, the great Emir Melek, rather better in future. You have lost a little battle—no, not a battle, a skirmish—but you have not lost the honor of a gentleman, because you were worsted by an overwhelming force—this force." And he slapped his holster. "Now, let us be friends. You must return your booty—give your slave girls to me, and I will see what amends I can make them for their sufferings. Perhaps I shall take some into my Palace service. Or, let's see, perhaps I could give you one or two as a token of esteem, a parting present .... Ha! who's this? I seem to know that face."

He was looking at Alis Carver. Poor, trembling Alis, pale under her golden tan—at last she had genuinely attracted the Count's interest. Nemon stepped forward and whispered to his master.

"Oh, *her* again!" said the Count, grimacing. "I thought I'd seen the last of that family. They're ill-omened. What, all the rest dead eh? Then let's make a clean sweep of them! Evidently I was too lenient with them before—and this is the Sword-god's way of telling me so. Barak, this girl you shall have, and anything you have taken from her house—and rest content with that."

Barak bowed gravely. "This is princely done, Lord Count. We Akhorians know how to be grateful." He extended his left hand. "Shall we be friends henceforth?"

The Count laughed. "I see I must learn some new customs. Very well, let us meet halfway." And, a little awkwardly, he took Barak's left hand in his right one, and the two of them achieved a curious palm-to-back-of-hand handshake. So strangely was pledged the alliance between Swordism and its former deadly enemy Lordism, the religion of "left-handed" or Invader life.

And then the pirates led away Alis, Cleito and Melissa, back to their ship. Before sunset, they were sailing out toward the mouth of Sabrina, and the open sea.

"That is a Count," said Cleito to Melissa, "than whom there can be no worse prince in all Atlantis, nay in all Dextra. May the Good Goddess take vengeance upon him for the Carvers, and for the children of Ringston!"

The nymphs were seeking their opportunity to speak to Alis, but it was difficult. Alis was being treated as a slave. The pirates, following the customs of Akhor, had removed her shoes, changed her garments for a short tightly belted green tunic and cut her hair short. But the nymphs were being treated as animals. Cleito had been naked to start with, and Melissa had had her sarong stripped off her. The pirate who did this had said:

"You will also serve us, creature, but do not pretend to be a person! That is an abomination unto our Law and our Lord. And see that you do not try to entice any man to lie with you, for in the day you do that, the man will be stoned to death—and you will be butchered, and your meat thrown to the monsters of the deep."

"Well," said Cleito, after he had gone, "I don't think there will be any Sir Hugos in Akhor."

She spoke lightly; but in truth the thought of Akhor filled her with horror. Akhor was a large island, bigger than the whole territory of Westria, lying in the Ocean southeast of Atlantis, halfway over toward the Isthmian shores of the World Continent. It had been conquered by the Livyan Saints during the Wars of the Seventh Century, and here there had sprung up pirate princedoms, now dominated by the High Emir Melek Sagan. The Akhorians had taken the Sifted Scriptures of the Saints and revised them again—restoring those parts of the Older Scriptures which the Sifters had rejected by reason of their barbarity. And with the Older Scriptures had come a return to older customs. For instance, the Livyans had insisted on monogamy, and still did so in their distant southern land; but the Akhorians now allowed the faithful up to four wives each, and unlimited numbers of concubines.

And Cleito was now remembering the many things that Estrild had told her of life in Akhor.

The Aknorians had reverted to the practice of human slavery. They made very little use of faun servants, as they regarded fauns with suspicion as "creatures of Lilith"—that is, of the Goddess. Nor could they have fed many, since they had destroyed most of the kin-vegetation of their island. There was no Agency monastery in Akhor; there had been one till the eighth century, but then the High Agent of Isthmia had closed it down when it was in danger of being infiltrated by Akhorian fanatics. Nor were there any coven-churches of the Sword of the Ring. Thus there was no intercessor for Atlantian captives in Akhor, no dilution of the bitterness of their slavery. Many emirs did not take men prisoners at all; others offered men slaves the choice of conversion to Lordism, or death. Women captives were used as slaves and as mothers of the next generation of Akhorian warrors.

It was growing dark now; the ships had their yard masts raised, and their sails spread to the full breeze, and they were moving out into the estuary. Already the ocean ahead was glowing with the bright phosphorescence of the Dextran sea-spark creatures, and a golden gleam in the west marked the place where the sun had gone down behind the eternal clouds. The rowers had stopped rowing, and were seated on the piles of shipped oars near the bulwarks, having their supper. The officers apparently were supping in greater state in the stern cabin.

Cleito and Melissa sat near the forward bow, hand in hand. No one was paying much attention to them—fauns were submissive creatures, who cared about two despised booty animals? They were not even being required to work.

"Melly," said Cleito seriously, "we'll have to be very brave when we're in Akhor. There will be no escape except by death—and perhaps that will not be long in coming to us. You know what Estrild said—how they slaughter fauns there for the slightest reason. But while we live, we should do our best to fight them. This world's a battlefield, and every little bit helps! We can help the human slaves—perhaps even act as spies. The Akhorians have many enemies, and *you* at least can communicate—"

"Mistress," whispered Melissa suddenly, "there is one calling to us."

"What?" said Cleito, looking around. "Where?"

"On the land. By a seashore. There is a message from a great one of power. It is the kind of call which fauns must obey."

And then a figure moved between them and the ship's side. There was a girl's voice, sobbing softly.

"Alis!" said Cleito quietly, jumping up. "Oh, Alis . . ."

Alis turned toward them. She recognized Melissa, and allowed Melissa to throw her green arms about her.

"O Goddess, Melissa," she wailed. "They—they are treating me like a faun! I had to wait a table for Barak."

"Is that all you had to do?" said Cleito grimly.

Alis sniffed. "I will be taken, too; but that comes later. They do everything in order, these men, according to their Law. Barak says he finds me pretty; and he only has three wives, so maybe I have a chance. But to be a wife I'll have to become a Lordist, and have my head shaved and my nails cut and weep for my father for a month in Akhor...."

"And you are willing to weep only for a month—and then marry him?" said Cleito, revolted. "The man who killed your mother and father and brother?"

"I don't want to," said Alis, beginning to sob again. "But what choice do I have? If I don't agree, I'll be no better than a faun."

"You *are* no better than a faun," said Cleito hotly. "In fact, you are worse."

"Mistress," said Melissa, touching Cleito's arm. "The call—it is stronger than ever. We are being commanded to cast ourselves into the sea."

"What!" cried Alis. "What are you talking about?"

"Be quiet," said Cleito. "Melly was speaking to me. Melly, is this call for Alis too?"

"It is for all captives. *Cast yourselves into the waters, and you will be borne up, and come safe home.*"

"Do you trust that call?" asked Cleito.

"Yes. It is the call of a greater one than I have ever heard. It is from the Mothers, or one high in the service of the Mothers. Of course I trust."

"Have you gone mad?" said Alis, raising her voice. A pirate growled at her. She continued more softly: "Melissa, you must be insane, and so is this other she-faun who speaks to me so rudely. I'm not going to jump into any sea. It's kilometers to the land already, and we'd be drowned."

"Alis, this is your last chance," said Cleito, as gently as she could manage. "Dear, you'll find this hard to believe, but I'm only a faun in appearance. I'm really and truly your cousin Cleito—I was saved from death by great powers. There *are* great powers in this world, and I believe they are trying to save us. If they say we will be borne up, then we *will* be borne up. And even if we're not, don't you think death would be preferable to what lies ahead of you? To be a slave concubine—or worse, to have to marry and pretend to love the man who murdered ... Alis, darling, please listen to me!"

"You're both mad, mad," said Alis hysterically, backing away and raising her voice. "I'll call my master—"

Melissa seized Cleito's arm. "Now—now!" she said.

THE WILDINGS OF WESTRON

Both girls leaped together. A pile of oars gave them the step up they needed, they reached the top surface of the rail, and then before the Akhorians could stop them, they were overboard.

The sea hit Cleito like a cold slap in the face—a very hard slap. Then she was going down, down into a world of ultramarine sparks. She could just see Melissa's slim shape as a blackness ahead of her, and she followed the nymph as she began to swim deep underwater. After a minute her lungs were bursting, and she came up to the surface just in time. She gasped in air, and looked around.

The ships were east of them, fairly clear in the last sunset glow, still quite close. There were men's heads above the rail of the one they had plunged from.

Then Melissa broke surface just before her, breathed, and ducked under again at once. She followed.

So they began their ducking escape. It worked perfectly; after a while, when they looked around it seemed to them that the ships had not even altered course. Why should they? Fauns were cheap animals; if two cared to drown themselves, it was hardly worth delaying the fleet.

But they *were* a long way from shore, and now it was becoming black night. Soon there would be no visible directions. If Melissa's strange "call" failed them, they would be utterly lost. . . .

And then suddenly Cleito realized that there were dark shapes all around them. With a shock of fear she wondered . . . sea monsters? Since she was not of native flesh, she might be an attractive morsel for any native ocean carnivore.

And then one of the strange shapes touched her on the arm, and a strange voice said:

"Hail, walker girlss! We willss see youss safely to landss . . ."

No, it couldn't be! But it was: another legend come true! These were merfolk—there were dozens of them, a whole shoal. She could make out their bodies a bit better now, for they were partly outlined by phosphorescence. They were basically human-shaped—or faun-shaped—but sleeker, rounder about the middle. They did not have tails exactly, but conjoined legs ending in wide double fin-feet;

their arms were short, and their heads were dumpy and rounded.

The merfolk rescued them very simply: one got under Cleito, another under Melissa, and they helped the girls to get comfortable astride, as though they were riding hexips. Then they began swimming steadily with powerful beats of their foot-fins, their heads going underwater for minutes at a time, only coming up with a rocking motion to blow and take in air at wide intervals.

Cleito marveled, and uttered thanks: thanks to the great Goddess, and to the sodality of Dextran creatures that worked together under—was it the Goddess? Or the Mothers? Or the planet Dextra itself? Perhaps these were all names for the same good power. . . .

Chapter
TEN

―――◆―――

The sea-things swam on through all of the night. After a while Cleito guessed that they were not making directly for the shore of Atlantis near Sabrina-mouth. On many nights of Dextra it is impossible to tell directions at all without a compass; but on this night of ocean adventure it happened that the brightest moon, Artemis, rose just as evening twilight ended, and her mild white halo in the high cirrus marked the southeast. Cleito realized that the merfolk were moving westward.

She soon became tired and hungry, since she had had an utterly exhausting day filled with tension and horror, and she had been given only scraps of food. She was cold too now, and leaned forward on her strange mount, partly drooping from exhaustion, partly bending for the sake of of the warmth she received from the merman's back. She certainly could not have swum this distance without help.

After a time she was only half conscious. She was moving through a dream world of dark silent shapes and innumerable gleams. Overhead were the dim haloes of two, then three moons stealing through the far cirrus, and below was a phosphorescent sky of points of light, bright ones close up and tiny ones dwindling away into infinite depths, like the *stars* that were celebrated in the old legends of Tellus. The upper sky was a layer of faint moony pearl, but the nether sky was a deep blue sapphire studded with living diamonds.

In the end she dreamed that she was flying through vacant interstellar space, riding a black metal ship. Under her knees, in the ship, were a hundred little people—the First Landers. She was their queen, and they were also her children; together they were going to find and populate a new world. Yes, and now they were reaching it, and it was a world with four pearly rings of moons, and it was named Atlantis, and her children were issuing out of that split-open ship, one hundred of them, all green fauns. . . .

She felt a jar, and came properly awake. A gray light was stealing over the world, the real world, abolishing the moon-gleams and fading the nether stars. Over to her left she could see the slim form of Melissa, riding steadily through the sea on her invisible merman. All around them were swirls, and dark backs parting the waters. Ahead there was a humpy unevenness on the horizon, and before that the foam of breaking waves.

In a few seconds there was a general disturbance. Round heads emerged from the water, snorting and blowing. Cleito found herself unceremoniously flung off the back of her ocean steed. She fell with a splash, but immediately her feet brushed a sandy bottom, and she stood. They were on a shoal, and she was within her depth.

Melissa was beside her, and took her hand.

"Be of good cheer, Mistress," she said. "We are nearly there."

The merfolk were taller than fauns, and some were now obviously standing upright on their flipper-feet, so that Cleito could at last get a clear view of at least their upper bodies. They were naked-skinned, hairless even on their rounded heads, and gray-blue in color; they had no external ears, their hands were webbed with folds of skin, but they still had four serviceable fingers. Their necks were very thick. It was quite impossible to tell males from females. But their faces were faun-faces somewhat distorted, and they had violet eyes.

The creatures stood in a ring around the two nymphs, blinking and puffing.

"Iss it well wiss you, little walkerss?" said one of the mermen, opening his eyes wide and holding out his paws. "One off yous we cannot feel insides."

"Oh, that'll be me," said Cleito, laughing wearily. "I'm all right, I think, if we haven't far to go." She could see

THE WILDINGS OF WESTRON

now a shoreline only a few hundred meters away, a yellow beach with purple trees beyond.

"Goods, goods," said the mermen. "Then the greats oness will be contents wiss uss."

And then in a flurry they were all gone. A forest of splashes, a swirl of water, and Cleito realized that their strange friends were swimming underwater, out to sea.

"What—what are they?" she asked Melissa. "They seemed to me like fauns—and yet not fauns. How could they be?"

"They are cousins of ours," said the nymph. "Once they were more like—they were blue-skinned fauns, small ones, but the Mothers changed them. They grew bigger, and rounder, and learned to eat fish, and so now they are merfolk."

"The Mothers do a lot of changing," said Cleito with a shiver.

"Yes. But always, they make better. The merfolk are wiser than the little blue fauns of old time. Come now, Mistress, we are waited for."

Cleito looked up—and there on the beach she saw a line of what seemed to be men, a dozen or so figures facing toward them. And now she could perceive something with her mental sense. It was like a beam of love, powerful love and reassurance. Following Melissa's lead, she waded forward, and then as the ground fell away she flung herself off the shoal and swam. The sea was calm, and quickly the two nymphs drew up to the shore, came aground again and stood up, bracing themselves against the strong gravity with which Dextra pulls her children to herself.

The men had waded a little way into the water to meet them. They were not alarming. They might have been Westrians except that most of them wore tunics of white linen and blue cloaks stamped with an unfamiliar badge, a large yellow wheel. But they were not ordinary men; Cleito knew at once that they were kin-people, eaters of native food. A word crossed her mind: *Wildings*—the legendary faunlike men of the Evenor Forest. But she could not attend to them now; it was their leader who fascinated her.

He was a bald-headed elder man with a short gray beard, brown-faced, dressed in a brown frieze jerkin and leather boots. At once a memory welled up in her—a memory charged with a confused, inexplicable emotion. It was partly shame, but partly something else, too.

"You—" she said, stumbling ashore and halting, her feet planted in the soft wet sand. "They called you Peders—"

"And they called you Chloe," said the brown Wilding in his powerful deep voice, "but neither was a true name." There was again that hard power coming out of his inmost being; but now he smiled, and said, "Fear not, good lady; your troubles are nearly over, I think. We are all friends here, and enemies to your enemies."

Cleito shivered. For the first time in this body she became conscious in almost human fashion that she was naked—perhaps because for the first time she was being treated as though she were truly a woman.

"And so you are," said the man who was not Peders, disconcertingly answering her unspoken thought. "The Mothers may translate, but they will never disrupt an intelligent creature's inmost being. In your deepest soul, Cleito, you will always be human. As for clothing, we will give you that if you wish. In any case you are cold, hungry, tired, I know. If you can walk a little way into the woods, we will find you a safe place to rest."

"There was a faun," said Cleito, knowing that her cheeks were darkening in the barely perceptible blush of a nymph. "You sold him—Wender—"

"He is safe," said Not-Peders. "I helped him escape from Alvern within two hours of your departure. And his true name was not Wender either. But we shall leave that for later. Now you must simply eat and rest."

Two of the Wildings covered Cleito and Melissa with their long blue cloaks, and then they all formed up around the nymphs like an honorable escort for human ladies of rank. They *were* an honorable escort: Cleito now saw that the men wore costly metal swords at their belts, and finely wrought steel brooches on their cloaks. They were conducting the girls toward the shelter of the purple woods.

"Where—where are we?" asked Cleito, as they reached the trees.

"In Evenor," said Not-Peders, "or just reaching it."

Cleito remembered that at some distance west of Sa-

THE WILDINGS OF WESTRON 109

brina-mouth, the forest of Evenor came down nearly to the sea. According to current beliefs in Westria, Evenor was a virgin forest, undisturbed at its core from the time before the First Landing a thousand years ago; and after the disasters of the seventh century, it had been allowed to spread. Indeed, the rulers of the various Free Counties of Atlantis had encouraged the growth of purple woods along their boundaries, partly as reserves for hunting native animals, and partly as "hedgerows" to define the frontiers of the princedoms. But Evenor was no mere hedge: it was a wild waste of wooded hills, in places over a hundred kilometers from east to west, and two hundred from south to north, with the ocean beyond it on the western side. And humans did not go into it; for some reason, it frightened them.

Cleito did not find it frightening at first. But as they plunged through the long blue grasses, and the purple tetron trees began to cluster more thickly, she began to perceive a curious mental tension. It reminded her of her "death"—the time when she lay in the boat-shaped petal of the Mother-Plant in the Agency courtyard—but this time the subtle knives were probing her *mind*, not her body. Melissa seemed to feel it too, for she reached out and took Cleito by the hand. Not-Peders said:

"Do not be afraid—you will not be injured. These are our defenders—they are much more terrible to left-handed life, such as ordinary humans. Look! There is one."

Cleito followed his pointing hand—and saw, in a shadowy clearing, a complicated shape, huge petals, a great central sphere.

"A Mother?" she whispered.

"Yes, but a warrior one. They mark the true frontier of Evenor. And now we are passing the line."

The knifelike mental sensation was decreasing, and finally it faded altogether.

They came at last to a glade of short blue grass, with a stream flowing through the edge of it, and small hillocks making the ground uneven, breaking it up into hollows like lairs or nests for giant birds. But the place was empty of animals, and very quiet; and the tetron trees of the glade edges spread their sprays far across, making a purple canopy that almost hid the cream-colored clouds.

"You may sleep safe here," said Not-Peders.

The nymphs chose one of the hollows and lay down. Then the Wildings brought them, apparently from some hidden store in the forest, kin-bread and nuts and sweet fruits, and in wooden cups pure water from the stream. And when they had eaten their fill, the men offered them as many cloaks as they needed for covering.

"Sleep now," said their leader.

Cleito needed no urging: she knew she was in good hands, and she fell asleep at once, with Melissa by her side.

Out of deep unconsciousness, she emerged slowly, with a sense of healthy well-being, into a twilight world. It was good to be a nymph, far from all nasty humans! She seemed to be lying on soft stuff—grass or hay—and to her joy she found that her lover was with her, her *mate*. He was a young boy faun, with dark brownish eyes, a handsome green face and lovely thick blue hair. They were already mates, and would be again: surely he would make her to bear little twin fauns or nymphs. She stretched out her hands to him.

"Wender," she murmured, "will you kiss me again, my love?"

And then the sky seemed to grow a shade brighter. This was no dream: she really was lying on grass, blue grass, and a mellow light was diffusing through the purple tree-canopy. A blue cloak had fallen off her shoulders, she was naked, and there was a naked green faun-boy bending over her, that handsome boy with very dark eyes.

There was no sign of Melissa, or the Wildings.

"What—what—" she gasped, shrinking back.

She felt utter confusion of spirit: she was both Chloe and Cleito at once, and her Cleito mind was fighting the impulse of her Chloe body to rush into the arms of this lusty young male faun, to give herself with mouth and sex to wild glorious lovemaking.

"No," she said, "no! I'm *Cleito*—"

"Oh, my love," said the boy, seizing her hand. He was half laughing and half weeping at once. "Of course you are! And I'm Will, your Will, Will the Wanderer who died-but-didn't-die by your side in the courtyard of the

Agency. And I was Wender too, at Alvern when you were still only Chloe and could not recognize me, and—Oh, Cleito, will you forgive me for what we did together there?"

Cleito stared at him. "O no, it can't be!"

"But it is," said Will. "Cleito, darling, didn't you have trouble too, convincing people—even your dear friend Melissa, at Avonside? Cleito, don't look with your eyes, let go—let your right flesh feel for you, reach out, don't speak. . . ."

Cleito did not speak; she relaxed, and her spirit went out and mingled with his spirit—and then she knew, beyond any shadow of doubt she knew, that this was indeed her own true love Will, Will the Wanderer, Will the Minstrel, who was a man in his central being though a faun in outward shape, for which reason, when he had been called Wender and she Chloe, she had not been able to read the thoughts of his mind. And now the forgotten words he had used on that delirious occasion came back to her clearly. Everything came back; he had called her Cleito even then, and she had not understood, but now she understood everything—or enough.

"Dear," said Will anxiously, letting go of her hand, "are you angry with me because I took advantage of you then? I am most truly sorry—"

Cleito laughed out loud. "Oh, Will, I'm not! Darling, I am not dishonored by that if you don't think so. You know she-fauns have no virginity to lose, and if they had I would still gladly lose mine to you."

Then they came together, embracing, kissing tenderly on the lips.

After a long, glorious moment Cleito drew away.

"Will," she said sorrowfully, "do you know what Sir Hugo did to me?"

"The other fauns told me," he said. "What of it? As you said, my dear, nymphs have no virginity. And anyway you couldn't help it, any more than you could about the Count—"

Cleito stared. "If you think that the Count. . . . Will, he didn't! I stopped him."

Will laughed shortly. "It wouldn't make the slightest difference if he had succeeded in raping you. We don't observe such superstitions in Evenor. Let's get back to important matters." He paused. "My dear—I don't know what to say. Fauns don't marry, but we are not truly fauns. *And*, my darling, listen: there's good hope that we will be able to regain our human shape sometime. If so, will you be my wife? I can tell you this: I have no other wife, and never will, for it's one wife only that is the custom of Wildings, and I am really a Wilding, and—will you marry me, Cleito?"

"Oh, my darling, of course!" said Cleito, kissing him again on the lips.

"Till then," said Will, "I—I don't quite know what to do."

"You don't?" said Cleito, laughing. "Well, I think I do. Let's try, anyway."

She put her tongue, her long nymph's tongue, deep into his mouth, and reached those centers of exquisite pleasure that only fauns, not humans, enjoy. The magic worked. Instantly Will seized her around her slim green waist, withdrew his mouth momentarily, and returned her probe with his own tongue. As he reached her little buds, her body responded. In seconds they were together, his boyness in her girlness; and the fiery circle of bliss, the true holy Ring, was coursing through their delighted bodies and their delighted spirits. For the pleasure this time was subtly different: it was equally intense, no whit less than when Chloe had made love as a mere innocent animal, but now in addition it was spiritual, intellectual. It was like the coupling of entities described in myths—a mating of bright, burning seraphim. Their minds were mating as well as their bodies; Cleito felt Will's delight in her, even as he felt her delight in him. Every minute particle and particular of their body-minds were commingling, from the head even to the feet, and on every plane of existence.

So they lay for a time that seemed timeless, infinite; and when at last they were returned into themselves, the sky was quite dark.

"Will," said Cleito, "where are we? Where are the others?"

"We are in Evenor," said Will, "and the others are nearby. Melissa is being cared for by Porphyry and the Knights of the Wheel; they will not intrude upon us till we call them."

"You will have to explain, my dear," said Cleito, smiling. "I think I have met the Knights of the Wheel, but who is Porphyry?"

"Porphyry Lee is the Hylist, the Lurker in the Woods—the chief of the Wildings in Evenor. He was known to you as the trader Peders. There is a real Peders, by the way, a trader in good favor with the Count—and I think he is going to get an unpleasant surprise when Sir Hugo calls on him and demands his three pieces of iron back! Porphyry took on the external shape of Peders for the sake of this mission—or rather, one of the Great Mothers altered him slightly. You will see him looking much more magnificent in his own shape when we get to Siderion."

"Really, Will!" said Cleito, with mock severity. "You must remember I've lost my pure faun ability to read minds! You'll have to tell me the whole story, beginning at the beginning. Dear, I don't even know who *you* really are, except that you were a fine minstrel and a bold mocker of that dreadful Count."

"Ho!" said Will. "There is much to tell. I don't know that I need say very much about myself, though."

She felt him move against her, then he was drawing a cloak over them both. Cleito snuggled against him in the darkness, and said, "Go on, Will. I *do* want to hear about you, darling."

"Well, I was born a Westrian, an ordinary human being like yourself, Cleito; but then, so were quite a few Wildings, quite a few Knights of the Wheel. I suppose you could say we are rebels; or as the Count would say, traitors. Well, you know what he does to traitors—or what he thinks he does! Luckily, the men in the Agency who study life science—they're on our side. Ambrose is of our party, and he has been encouraging the Count to indulge in 'flayings,' of course because this is really a way of escape. The condemned rebels become fauns—and afterwards, if all goes well, they become Wildings—men and women again, but men and women of 'right' flesh, eaters of native food whose home is the great forest we are in now."

"But," said Cleito, "if that Mother Plant can change us so much, why doesn't it turn us into Wildings directly?"

"Because there are two sorts of Mothers," said Will. "The kind in the Agency is a hardy sort—a Warrior. It can survive when shut in a city building, or fixed in a cold place, whereas the true Great Mothers cannot. The Great Mothers are highly intelligent, and versatile—within wide limits they can turn living creatures into many different shapes, and from Invader-flesh to native-flesh and back *as they choose*. Five hundred years ago, according to our traditions, there were only Great Mothers on Dextra. They are a kind of plant-animal whose first home was far east of here in a country called Anthis or New Asia. Do you know that old story, the Tale of the Turners?"

"Yes," said Cleito. "But I thought it was a fable."

"Sometimes fables are literally true. This tale is one example. We have an authentic written copy of it, a book printed on an old hand press in the sixth century, the author being one Endymion Lee; he was a direct ancestor of Porphyry. You remember how in that tale Endymion's father, the old wizard Lucius Lee, wandered off into an eastern forest to be a sort of High Priest of the forest Power? That is where the tale breaks off. Well, in our version the Power is shown to be actually the Great Mothers. And our traditions tell us what happened afterward. A few years later, Lucius came secretly to New Europe, to take charge of the new Mothers growing there beyond the frontiers of the human settlements, and in that area he and other members of the Lee family set up the Fellowship of the Wheel. The Wheel, I must tell you, is the true center of our various groups and organizations. Some are secret, others not. Your Ring Church, for instance, Cleito—it's not secret, but it's the outer circle of the Wheel, nevertheless."

Cleito gasped. Will laughed.

"Yes. These are great secrets, Cleito—they have been kept for four hundred years. One of our fears is that they won't last much longer—but perhaps that won't matter. Now, let me get back to my story.

"The Ring Church was founded by secret members of the Wheel in the late sixth century to combat the influence of the Lordist Saints, and in that it succeeded—too well, perhaps. The Ringers converted most of New Europe, and then some extreme Ringers—not Wheel members—they went further, and founded the Sword Church. By the next century the human world was split into two hostile camps, the Saints versus the rest, each armed with laser weapons—with the inevitable result. Luckily, by then secret Wheel members had entered the Science Agency, and in the time of the Wars they controlled it sufficiently to save the world from utter destruction. For one thing, they had eliminated atomic energy."

"What's that?" said Cleito, bewildered.

"Frankly, I don't know. Even the knowledge of it was suppressed by the eighth century physicists. I think it was like lasers and poison combined. Meanwhile, the main Hub of the Wheel was growing, far in the interior of the continent, sheltered from the Wars. Our folk there had no faith in physical weapons, and no wish to use them themselves. They had hoped to win over the human world gradually, peacefully, bringing good men to the Mothers and changing them into kin-flesh, into Wildings. You know why this is necessary—kin-flesh has this special power of mental sympathy, and that keeps down to a minimum. But our people miscalculated. The human population was growing too fast, and so was their physical weaponry. The Wheel folk would have been at the mercy of violent men, unless they developed powerful defenses themselves.

"So, through the Mothers, they did. The Great Mothers modified some of their own spores, and produced the specialized Warrior Mothers. These had enormously increased powers of mental attack, which could be released or checked by their human allies, those who were trained to command them. But the Warrior Mothers paid a price—they lost the power of handling words, and most of their ability to transform animals. Now they can do only one operation of that sort—the thing that was done to us. They can turn out green fauns—nothing else."

"What happens if ordinary humans try to pass the Warrior Mothers?" asked Cleito. "There's a line of them around Evenor, isn't there? What happens if there's an invasion? Are the men killed?"

"Not quite," said Will. "The Mothers object to killing

rational creatures—they gave up doing that *millions* of years ago. No, the Warriors—well, they *disable* them. The victims will recover, in a matter of weeks, if they are properly cared for. But they are definitely out of any immediate battle!"

"And the other Mothers," said Cleito, "the Great Ones. Where are they?"

"There are some in many parts of the world now," said Will, "but only in dense warm purple forests. There are some in Evenor—and these, I hope, will give us back our human shape. But I must tell you, dear, that there's a limit to the number of times a person can be changed through the Mothers. One gets weaker in the end, and it becomes dangerous. Porphyry tells me I may go through only one time more."

"Why," said Cleito, pressing his hand in the darkness, "how often have you been through, Will?"

Will laughed. "Several times, my dear. You see, I have been spying on the Count for our party, and I suppose I have been too careless. So I have been a faun before. I think you have seen my cast skin already."

"No!" said Cleito, horrified. "Who—"

"On Westgate," said Will, "there is exhibited a certain traitor-page called Rondel. I protest, Cleito, I was *not* caught in the arms of a concubine, I really was a genuine, wicked, political traitor."

"Oh good Goddess!" cried Cleito, clutching him. "My love, my love, you must not do such things again, not take such risks!"

"Why then I will not," said Will, with a merry laugh. "My dear, now at least for a time we shall lie low. When we fight the Count again, I think it will be openly."

"Will," said Cleito, "there is still one thing you haven't told me—not sufficiently. Who *are* you?"

"My surname is Turner—same as the former Counts, but don't be alarmed, you don't have to curtsy to me, darling! You know it's a common name in Atlantis, though maybe less common in Westria since the Conquest, because people with that name have been changing it for political reasons. Well, I was born in Westron, but all my family died when I was young. I was brought up by some good friends." He paused, and laughed. "Don't you think we've talked enough of these serious matters? *I* slept most of today, too, just like you—Porphyry insisted on it—but the others must be tired, and we won't be moving on till dawn. This night is for us, Chloe—sorry, I mean Cleito—"

"Let me be Chloe for once—once again," said Cleito, throwing her arms around her lover.

They slept a little again before dawn, and then, when the light was golden-gray, the chorus of handibirds woke them. A wild sphinx took off from a nearby tetron tree, scattering the kin-birds like a shower of multicolored shrieks.

"It's time," said Will, smiling, kissing Cleito on the tip of her green snub nose as she opened her eyes, and smoothing back her blue hair.

He led her to the other glade, a few hundred meters up the little stream, where Porphyry, Melissa and the Wheel Knights had been camping. There were other creatures in that clearing too. At first, Cleito thought they were hexips tethered to the trees; next she thought they were men mounted on hexips; but that was wrong, too, the "riders" were seated much too far forward. She uttered a cry.

"Dear, don't be afraid," said Will. "They're friends, too. Everything in Evenor is friends. They are one type of—centaur."

"But senties are small," said Cleito, staring. "These—they're huge!"

"I said *centaurs*, not senties. Oh yes, they're related. In fact, there are many kinds of centauroids. These ones we call Myrmies. They're not very bright, but they do speak. They serve us instead of hexips—also as a sort of mobile Warriors."

Cleito stared at the creatures. They stood as tall as a man mounted on a hexip, and they were covered in blue-gray fur. Their heads were rounded at the back in almost human fashion, but they had long muzzles and catlike eyes with yellow eyeballs. There was a curious solemnity about their stare, their thin blue lips. They had four powerful-looking legs ending in massive hoofs, and also muscular arms and broad hands. Their four fingers ended in short claws. And—an oddly grotesque touch—these handy beasts were *saddled*.

There were over a dozen of them. And several of the Knights were on foot beside them, stroking them, brushing their coats, *talking* to them.

Will laughed at Cleito's consternation. "We're going to ride them to Siderion. You'll see, it's quite easy! Easier than staying on a hexip. If you start swaying in your saddle, your Myrmie will put up his hands behind his forebody and help you to stay on. They're really obliging beasts."

"But they look so—fierce!"

"They *are* fierce—when they have to be. Not to us. But you should see them hunt! I'm afraid they're not vegetarians. Maybe I should tell you, dear, that they're another development produced by the Great Mothers. The Hylists asked for a sort of super warhorse, for use in emergencies, and the Mothers took a smallish centauroid and—this is the result."

Now all the Wildings were awake; Porphyry took Will aside, and Melissa came up to Cleito. She was smiling, and Cleito was aware of her loving joy.

"Oh, my dear Mistress, I am so glad about Master Will—"

"Melly," said Cleito severely, "there is one thing you have got to stop."

"What?" said Melissa anxiously. "Have I offended ye, Mistress?"

"Only in calling me Mistress. *That* you must stop! I am a nymph, Melly, a nymph like you. We are friends, sisters. Call me Cleito, please, or any variant of that you please—nothing else!"

"Well—but you are not *quite* like me—Cleity," said Melissa with a smile.

PART III:

Countess and Queen

Chapter
ELEVEN

They were a strange company in a strange place—three fauns, a dozen Wilding knights, the Hylist Porphyry Lee, and sixteen semi-intelligent centaurs, all in a glade of blue grass surrounded by the purple trees of Evenor. And they had a journey of two days' rugged travel ahead of them to reach Siderion, capital of the Knights of the Wheel.

Before they started, Will introduced Cleito formally to the Knights: to Ferbrand, Val, Kyot, Kurwen, Valmont, Erec, Urians, Clesian, Mark, Durald, Tristan and Kay.

"We don't use surnames much in Evenor," said Will, "because we have rather too few of them. Out of the forty-odd original surnames of the world, we don't seem to have collected more than twenty. Ferbrand is a Lee, Kyot is your namesake a Dixon, Fal is an Anders, and Mark of course is a Turner like me. And so forth."

"Don't worry, Lady Cleito," said Ferbrand. He was a young man of some twenty-five years, brown-haired with greenish eyes. "You'll soon sort us out. The ones with the short plain names are mostly the Changelings—Val and Mark and Kay—and of course, your Will." He paused, his green eyes oddly mirthful. "The rest of us were 'born wild,' as we say. Our families have been established here for generations, some for centuries. I am wildborn myself."

Cleito gathered from Will's manner that Ferbrand was his special friend, and now the Knight showed himself concerned to look after not only Will, but also Cleito and

Melissa. He found them each a Myrmie-centaur to ride, and then said:

"What about clothes? We have a tunic and a pair of riding trews for you, Will—special ones, boy-sized for your new little form—but we weren't expecting you'd have company; we could only get the extra Myrmies at the last moment."

"Oh, we two don't need anything," said Cleito, looking at Melissa. Her first shyness had worn off. According to the Wildings, there were many free-ranging fauns in Evenor, and they normally wore no clothes at all, except when they dressed up for special occasions.

"Very well," said Ferbrand, "but I shall make sure you borrow a cloak, Lady Cleito, in the evenings. It gets cold in the hills."

Cleito found she had to ride her Myrmie astride, like everyone else—ladies were not expected to go sidesaddle in Evenor—and she was soon thankful for this. She was frighteningly higher off the ground than she would have been on a hexip, and the Myrmie moved faster, but luckily with a smoother, less wriggling motion, and she had his forward torso to hang onto when necessary.

What was a little unnerving at first was that her mount kept making *remarks*.

"Steady does it, little 'un—needn't dig yer knees in so much, greenie—ho no, *not* around me neck . . ." He had a curious gruff, almost barking voice.

"I hope I'm not hurting you," said Cleito as she dropped back into the saddle.

"Not you," he rumbled. "Myrmie can carry much more weight than *that*. Not to signify."

"What's your name?" she asked.

"Myrmie," said the Myrmie, clearing a small brook with one easy leap.

"I know, but what's your *own* name?"

This seemed to puzzle her mount. "We are all Myrmie," he growled, and lapsed into a stolid silence.

Will, riding by her side, called to her, "They haven't got individual names. In fact, they're hardly individuals at all. It's even more drastic than the shared life of fauns. The Handlers can tell them apart, I think, but I'm not sure that the Myrmies themselves can."

"Who are the Handlers?"

"Another race of centaurs—fully intelligent ones. You'll see some at Siderion."

They made good progress for the first hour, heading northward, and then the ground began to rise toward the first range of hills, those that surrounded the main bulk of Evenor, shutting it off from the Sabrina valley on the east, from the Free County of Camlan on the north, and from the Ocean south and west. The purple forest was very thick on the foothills, but they were following a beaten trail, a blue grass road overarched by sprays of tetron and mandrake and paraquerc. The forest was full of life—little senties and kin-deer at ground level, and handibirds, sphinxes and bat-monkeys in the treetops. A couple of times that day they caught glimpses of wild fauns, who emerged from tall blue bushes and waved as the myrmicade trotted past. Melissa made a point of waving back. Turning to Cleito after one such encounter, she laughed.

"This is the Good Place, Cleity,' she called.

"What do you mean, Melly?"

"We have always known of it," said Melissa, "we who were servants of men in the Free Counties. We knew there were fauns who were not called by the Mothers to be bought and sold by men, to be beaten or ill-used; and we knew that their place was not far away. It is here! These fauns are telling me how they live: sometimes they go to Siderion and serve the Wildings, but they do that for pure friendship, since the Wildings are *kin*, brothers, and also protectors of Evenor. And there are other kinsfolk in Evenor, beautiful ones—and we shall see them soon."

They halted for the midday meal in a glade on a small plateau. They could have lived off the country, since there were many kin-fruit and nut trees in the area, but the Knights had adequate supplies in their saddlebags. A nearby stream, cold and clean, provided them with drink.

The weather was extraordinary: the clouds were thinner than Cleito could ever remember, with patches of *blue* among the white cirrus. And then it happened: a blinding yellow-white disc sailed out into the empty blue. The First Landers had called it Delta Pavonis, but now, after a thousand years, all Dextrans called it merely the Sun. A

Clearance, a Manifestation, may happen once in ten or twenty years; Cleito had never seen one before.

Will held her hand as they both turned their heads away from the blinding disc and saw the glade transfigured in that hard, pitiless light which divided all things into nearly white brightness and nearly black shadow. The Wheel Knights had dropped to their knees, their heads bowed as though in prayer; Melissa was hiding behind a tree; but Porphyry stood very much erect, his face raised to the sky, his hands outstretched. Cleito could sense that he too was praying, in some fashion.

When it was over, and the glory had faded, he turned to them.

"One day," he said quietly, "something else will break through those clouds, something which will come to us from another Sun."

"What—" began Cleito fearfully.

"It will be a metal ship," said Porphyry, "and I think there will be men in it, for we are not the only men in the Universe. A thousand years is a goodly time to recover from most disasters, perhaps the tale of Tellus is not yet all told. And there were other great ships that went out from Tellus, seeking other stars than ours. And in the day when they come—may we be ready to receive them! If they have not learned wisdom by their sufferings, we may then have a much more terrible war to wage. But—sufficient for now is our own evil. Let us go on."

When they made camp that first evening, Cleito suddenly became aware that Porphyry was no longer with them.

"He is riding ahead," said Will. "He is going to prepare a reception for us. Also, he is going to get himself changed—into his own true shape. The forest called Matrum, where the Great Mothers live—it's only a sort way west of Siderion."

They were standing a little apart from the others, on the fringe of a wide glade. Cleito said, "O Will, shouldn't we be going to the Mothers too?"

Will looked sad. "I will take you there as soon as you like, my love. But Porphyry has told me that I myself must not—not go through again for at least another month. By then I should have recovered my strength, and it will be safe for me."

Cleito said, "Then I will not go through either, till you do. What! How could I become a human girl while you were still a faun! Will, you—you wouldn't even *fancy* me—no more than Narses did, or Modo or Mahu when I was human."

Will smiled. "It's not quite as bad as that here. Don't forget, we're all kin-flesh! There's not a single living thing in Evenor which is otherwise. The 'humans' are all Wildings, and so shall we be—and *our* fauns and kin-humans smell all right to each other, and sexual love between them is not unknown. It's not common, but it's not forbidden, either. Nothing is forbidden in Evenor except cruelty. So it *would* be possible for us, my dear."

"But it wouldn't work very well—would it?" said Cleito. "no circuit."

"No," said Will. "Cleito darling, you realize, don't you, that when we both go through, we will still lose that? Love between Wilding men and women is good, it's glorious because there is mental mingling—but the circuit-pleasure is something which only fauns can know."

Cleito pondered. At once she was tempted: why *ever* be a human again? Fauns were in so many ways better-designed animals—truly designed, for they had been deliberately evolved by the Mothers, in the early sixth century, to satisfy a human archetype. They could run better than humans, their pleasures were enormous, in sex they had no shame. As for giving birth . . .

"Will," she said, "do we *have* to go through?"

Will grasped her hand. To her surprise, she found that his grip was not steady. His dark faun eyes looked deeply sad.

"*You* don't have to, Cleito," he said. "But sooner or later, I will have to. I have certain obligations to my people."

"Your people? Do you mean the Wildings?"

"Er—yes. And the whole Fellowship of the Wheel, including the fauns of Westria and the humans there of our own party—and many others. There is going to be a war, my dear—sooner or later an open war. If I and my friends get our way, really quite soon. And at that time, I must be in human shape. It is expected of me, and—I suppose you might say, I expect it of myself."

"And it will never be safe for you to change back again—to this shape?"

"No."

Cleito threw her arms around Will and kissed him lightly on the lips. "My darling, forgive me my weakness! I have been so afraid as a human—once I was a faun, well, it's true I was a slave or less than a slave, but somehow nothing mattered so much. Fauns are *ignored*. It would be so nice to be a faun forever in Evenor, their Good Place; and of course there's the pleasure, too."

"I understand," said Will dully. "Well, Cleito, we can be mates for a time, while I am in this shape, but then—"

"Oh shut up, you fool," cried Cleito. "Do you think I would leave you? Will, I'll be a human, even a mind-blind Invader human if it's necessary for us. When it's your time to go through, I'll go too. Come to that," she added, "I don't think it's right for us to be faun-changelings for ever. In the heart of us, we're hunans—sad creatures, perhaps, but I think the Goddess, or whatever is higher than the Goddess—the truth of things—would wish us in the end to be our own true selves. Improved a little, maybe, but ourselves."

Will kissed her fervently. "Nothing can come between us now," he said. "And in the meanwhile—"

"In the meanwhile," laughed Cleito, "let us gather tubolia buds while we may." And she led him out of the camp into the deep purple shade of the forest.

On the second day they descended a little at first, through hills covered with red flowering kin-gorse, and came out onto a rolling blue-and-purple plateau with stretches of grass punctuated with scattered trees or thicker woods. On the open savannahs they several times encountered herds of native large game—mostly cervoids, big six-legged antlered beasts that scattered and fled at their approach. Cleito perceived a certain restlessness in her steed.

"Myrmie eats those," he said once, looking around with a wild gleam in his yellow eye.

Indeed, she had noticed that the Knights fed their mounts on strips of dried meat.

And then on one occasion, as they came out of a wood, they suddenly saw a hunt in progress. There were unsaddled Myrmies rushing around the flanks of a cervoid herd—and there were a different sort of centaurs running behind, and seeming to direct the Myrmies.

"Handlers," called Will, pointing.

The new centaurs were smaller than Myrmies, and they were astonishingly human-looking—in fact, thought Cleito, if humans were four-legged, they would look like *that*! Their heads were, quite simply, the heads of young men—and women, for there were a couple of girl-centaurs among them. They were all black-haired, brown-skinned, and their feet ended in toes, not hoofs. Their tails were black, too, and seemed like a repetition of their head hair. They were naked except for a few straps and belts which supported various pouches and sheathed swords and daggers; thus Cleito saw, with amazement, that their sex organs were situated, human-fashion, between their front legs, unlike every other six-limbed animal of Dextra.

Will looked at Cleito and laughed. "They're also a kind of Wilding," he said. "Do you remember the Tale of the Turners? These are the descendants of Kimon and Helen, that boy and girl who preferred to go on four legs—and the Mothers changed them according to their wish, and their children bred true."

"They look very *wild*," said Cleito.

The human-centaurs were all brandishing throwing spears, even the girl-centaurs; they laughed as they ran after their Myrmies, their dark eyes agleam with the fury of the chase. Then the hunt was gone, vanished among the trees of the next wood.

"Porphyry has taught us to control their wildness," said Will. "I think it will come in useful, soon."

The second night they camped on a high hillside in a wood of black-needled spinifers. The air was cold and misty, and Cleito was glad to sleep in Will's arms well wrapped in a couple of blue cloaks. On the third morning they pushed on between shaggy hills, their mounts laboring up a punishing rise. The Wilding Knights looked at Will.

Even though he was outwardly a mere faun, Cleito noticed that they treated him as their leader. Will raised his hand, and brought it down sharply. At this signal, the Myrmies were halted and everyone dismounted. But the steeds did not have to be led as the party plodded forward; they merely followed their masters, drawn up in good order like a troop of cavalry.

Soon they were out of the woods and climbing the final rise of a blue grassy hill, one of a line of downs that barred the view northward. The air was chill. High up against the golden clouds twittered an invisible kin-lark.

At last they were really at the top. And Cleito caught her breath. Below them, northward, lay a blue parklike plain set in blue hills on every side. The great hollow must have been twenty-five kilometers in diameter. In places there were gleams of water, and beside them the tiny block-like shapes of buildings; in other places, dotted trees merged into compact woods with trim edges as though they had been artificially planted. To Cleito's astonishment, these trees all had blue, not purple leaves; and the nearest of them, at the foot of the hill on which they stood, looked eerily familiar in their spreading shapes. But what held her eye most was a building in the midst of the plain. There were stretches of water to right and left of it, with tiny white dots on the water. The building itself shone like a sapphire sparkling on the summit of that central hilly island. It was far, far away beneath and ahead of them, and yet because of its dramatic positioning and amazing brightness, it impressed its presence on that whole strange valley.

"Siderion," said Will, with awe in his voice. "The Palace of the Hylist, the Castle of the Wheel."

"Those trees," said Cleito, looking down at the foreground. "Why are they *blue*? They look just like oaks!"

Will laughed. "They *are* oaks—of a sort! You might call them Wilding oaks. They are as much oaks as these Knights of ours are humans. They were planted in this valley from acorns which had been passed through the Great Mothers—changed over to kin-life. This valley is full of changeling trees—blue oaks, blue beeches and so on. The only original-native trees and plants we've got here are food-bearers—and they've been planted too. Be-

THE WILDINGS OF WESTRON 129

cause, in the seventh century, this whole valley was overwhelmed by a disaster, its original native life nearly wiped out."

"A death-weapon attack?"

"No. This was death from the sky. Porphyry says it must have been a complete coincidence. A huge meteor struck the middle of Evenor—it blasted a crater which is now that central lake, and threw up the island in the middle. Luckily it occurred right in the middle of the Second War, so the people of Atlantis didn't notice—they felt the earthquake, of course, but thought it was some kind of enemy action. Actually, there was more than one meteorite. Others came down a bit further north, masses of nickle-iron—"

"*Iron!*" cried Cleito. "Have you been able to find them?"

"Yes! We're rich in iron, my dear—iron from the sky! Haven't you noticed that all our friends here have steel swords? We've hardly even had to mine the stuff—there was a huge lump lying on the surface at Ferrol, which is just beyond that blue horizon; and there are smaller pieces still being found in Siderion itself."

"Will," said Cleito, staring, "if the Count only knew about this—"

"He'd try to invade us, of course; the whole world would! Well, let them try: the result might surprise them."

"The Count has the death-weapon," said Cleito.

"Yes, there is that," said Will. "That was a most unlucky chance for us. Or was it? Porphyry has a saying—'He that uses Death will find that Death will use him.'"

As they rode down the hill Cleito pondered the wonderful history of Evenor. Will and Ferbrand had told her how the first Wildings had established themselves here as far back as the sixth century, well before the Laser Wars. The first Great Mother was transported to this wilderness from the Province of Classica by a man named Benjamin Turner, a man with a strange personal history, for he had been conceived as a Wilding, born as an ordinary human, and then in his twenties had cast himself into the first Great Mother to grow in Atlantis and so had become a Wilding again, and the first Hylist of Evenor. Ben Turner was the eldest son of the half-legendary Turners, Mark and Meriam; he was also a collateral ancestor of the former Princes of Westron, the Turner Counts who had been massacred by Horold and the Trinovantians twenty years ago. Ben had left direct descendants in Evenor. The present generation of Wildings did not care much for the ideas of hereditary rank or autocracy, but if it were expedient to oppose Count Horold with a "legitimate" heir, they could easily find one.

Toward the end of the seventh century, a generation after the Laser Wars, Evenor had finally been sealed off from the rest of Atlantis with the chain of Warrior Mothers. And there were other Hylist strongholds elsewhere on Dextra—in particular the great forest of Endor in the center of the World Continent. Here was Rotaris, the capital of the Wheel, the foundation of Lucius Lee himself. But of that place, Ferbrand and Will had spoken very little; they seemed not entirely happy about it.

Now they were down among the trees, and Cleito looked about her with delight. Blue grass, blue woods, blue-leaved oaks and beeches and hornbeams and ash and thorn, with here and there evergreens—or should they be called "everblues"? There were dark-blue laurels and rhododendrons—the place was like a Wilding gentleman's park. There were even Wilding or Changeling animals, deer and squirrels and birds which looked just like Invader animals and birds but simply could *not* be.

"Are there also Wilding fish in the lake?" called Cleito to Will as they cantered along.

"How did you guess?" grinned Will.

The valley of Siderion also held many intelligent creatures. At times they caught sight of green fauns and nymphs, most of them cheerfully naked, but one or two in blue or red or yellow waist-cloths, and many of both the clothed and the naked ones had stuck bright flowers in their blue hair behind their pointed ears. The fauns waved as the cavalcade cantered by, and the Knights and Will and Melissa and Cleito waved back.

After a while they were riding down a road—or what passed for a road in Evenor. It was a wide grassy track between soaring blue elms, and at the end of the avenue glittered the waters of the crater lake. Beyond again, the

THE WILDINGS OF WESTRON 131

walls of the palace-castle sparkled and flashed like the facets of a blue-green jewel.

"What's it made of?" gasped Cleito.

Will smiled. "Glass. Bricks of glass! You can't see through the walls, but they let in a lovely light. And they're quite as strong as stone."

"You must have some marvelous workmen."

"So we do," said Will. "Only they're not men. They're another race of fauns—*blue* fauns with purple hair. Their ancestors used to be called Gobblers, but these gobblers of ours are bigger than the old sort, and stronger and cleverer. They are our miners and metalsmiths and builders—they love those kinds of work. And other kinds, too, you'll see."

They came to the end of the avenue and dismounted by the shore of the lake. Close by stood a wooden house with a tiled roof, with a pier or jetty beside it going out into the lake, and at the jetty was a barge or small galleass, equipped with both sail and oars. There were people all about now, both green fauns and Wilding humans, and they welcomed the newcomers with courteous greetings such as one bestows on old friends.

Now for the first time Cleito saw Wilding women—but she thought "ladies" was the better word for them. They could have passed for Westrians, except that many of them had green or blue eyes—and all were dressed in gay outlandish costumes, a bewildering variety of styles, some in long dresses, some in very short ones, some even in trousers. There was an equally great range of footwear, and one or two sported absurd-looking tall caps. Thus it came home to Cleito most vividly that these people were a *nation*: they were not Westrians, they had their own traditions reaching back hundreds of years, and for that matter the Evenor-born Wildings had a trace of a different accent, soft and lilting.

Sweet-spoken ladies were greeting the newcome Knights. Urians had a wife here, Kyot a sweetheart. And one young woman of perhaps twenty-five years, a lady in a very form-fitting gown, a jeweled collar and pointed, turned-up shoes, came up to Ferbrand, kissed him, and then turned a sorrowful gaze on Will.

"Can it be—you?" she said softly. "Dearest boy, Porphyry warned us, but—"

"Yes, it is really me, Jacynth," said Will. "I hope the shape does not offend you."

Jacynth wrinkled her fine nose. "It is not what I would wish for my gallant prince."

Will put out his hand at once, as though he meant to lay his green fingers on her lips. "But I am no prince, Jacynth, only a poor Changeling, and when I was in more human shape in Westria they used to call me Will the Wanderer; and so I would like to be called here also."

Jacynth gave a tinkling laugh. "I lost track of your names, my dear. Rondel, now, that was a sweet one, and a sweet boy you were then, I remember. I hope at least you will not deny your surname, Will Turner."

"Come now," said Will hastily to Cleito. "The barge is waiting for us."

They all went out on the pier and boarded the little ship. It was manned by Wilding rowers, young men in short blue tunics, and a mixed crew of fauns and Wildings to manage the helm and ropes and sail. Soon they were moving out into the lake. But Cleito had lost interest in the ship and the scenery. As soon as she could get Will to herself, away from his various Wilding friends, she said:

"Will—who is Jacynth? I mean—" she hesitated—"is she something special to you?"

She looked down the barge to where Jacynth was standing arm in arm with Ferbrand, and talking laughingly with Celsian and Erec.

Will laughed and ruffled Cleito's blue hair. "Jacynth bears the great surname of Lee. She is a very sprightly lady of Siderion, and very popular. And she *has* been a friend of mine in the past—but also of a great many other young Wilding knights. You have nothing to fear, my darling Cleito. No, she is nothing *special* to me. There is no one but you."

Ferbrand had torn himself away from Jacynth, and now he came up. "Will," he said, his green eyes serious, "I have just heard—Symmachus is here."

"The Legate of Endor?" said Will. "What does he want?"

"Delay," said Ferbrand.

THE WILDINGS OF WESTRON

There was a regular harbor at the shore of the island, and when they landed they found the quays and the blue grassy shores thronged with inhabitants of several species. There were Wildings wearing the badge of the Wheel, and green fauns, and also the strange, stocky Gobblers whom Will had described—blue-skinned fauns with purple hair not only on their heads but also all over their legs and almost up to their waists. They seemed to be busy on tasks connected with the building or refitting of ships. Also among the welcomers were a couple of human-centaurs, a male and a female, dressed in purple cloaks, but nothing else. Finally, there was one person who stood in a group of green fauns, but stood taller than any faun Cleito had seen. His skin was bright gold and his hair green, and he wore a gorgeous gold-and-purple cloak and a diadem of blue laurel.

"Oh my!" said Melissa, staring. "Isn't he handsome! What is he?"

"We call them Silvans—or sometimes just Gods," said Will, smiling. "They are a sort of faun royalty, and they have their own capital, too, in the next valley. It is a tradition among us—a prophecy, if you like—that one day Evenor will be *their* kingdom when we Wildings have moved on elsewhere. This fellow, by the way, is Silvius himself—the High King. He does us great honor by coming down to welcome us here."

Silvius now came forward. He surveyed Will a trifle critically.

"Well," he said, "Master Turner: some would aver that this was a sad change for you. Our own opinion is that you are now decidedly more handsome, even though a mere greenskin. But welcome, in any shape—welcome back to our realm of Silvania!"

Then they all plodded up the slope to the Glass Castle.

The building, or rather complex of buildings, had one pecularity, striking enough even among many others—it was built on a spiral plan, perhaps to lessen the effort of climbing to its highest level. Once inside the shining gateway, they turned to their left and began ascending between translucent blue-green walls. Cleito soon realized that the whole palace was very large—Will explained that it was both a princely court, and a sort of monastery, and much else besides, and the outbuildings contained sleeping quarters for thousands of guests, servants, Knights, ladies, and people of other categories and of various species. They had made a complete circuit of the central hill before they reached the doorway of the main cylindrical building, and entered the splendid Hall of the Hylist.

Here at last Cleito felt more or less at home, for the hall was like others she had known, including that of the Palace of Westron. But everything was bathed in the bluish light which diffused through the glass-brick walls. It was a little like being underwater—say, in a crystal-clear shallow sea.

And directly ahead of them, among many Knights at the center of the high table, sat a handsome elderly man in a blue robe. He had a trim beard of reddish brown sprinkled with gray, and fine long auburn hair. It was quite impossible to guess his age: he was surely at least fifty, but his brow was smooth, and there was hardly a wrinkle about the corners of his eyes. The irises of his eyes were surprisingly dark.

"Welcome—Will," he said in a strong voice—a voice which was almost familiar, being deep and resonant. "And you too, Lady Cleito, and you, little Melissa. My lord Silvius has already done you honor, but now let me add my poor greeting. Welcome all, to Siderion!"

Cleito knew that this must be Porphyry the Hylist, he who had saved her from the Akhorian pirates and welcomed her on the shore. But with the change of face there had also been some change of voice. Once more she was shaken at the thought of the powers wielded by those mysterious Mothers.

"And now," said Porphyry, "when you are bathed and rested, my friends, we shall celebrate this night a great feast. We have happily passed great dangers, and there will be dangers to face again; but tonight we shall make pause from such, a grateful holiday for us all."

Chapter
TWELVE

Will and Cleito were given a room in the second story of the great glass-brick cylinder, with a window facing east over the outbuildings, the lake and the plain of Siderion. There was a neat bed at floor level in one corner, and a shower cubicle in another. There was also a shaded glass globe which Will told Cleito was an electric light.

"Why," said Cleito, with a little shudder, "it reminds me of my cell in the Count's palace. But no bars on the window this time! No, it's not really like that cell. O Will, how marvelous, our first *room* to share! But it's a strange one—so *light!*"

She looked around. There were small holes high up the walls for ventilation, so that the place was airy, not hot. The ventilator holes carried sounds from adjoining rooms—murmurs of conversation, light laughter. Privacy was therefore not total; but in the nature of kin-beings, it could not be. All "right" flesh had this property of sympathy, and Will and Cleito couldn't help being aware of personalities all around them—some human, some fauns—all creatures of good will. They were faintly aware, among others, of Melissa: she was not far away, for she had been given a bed among King Silvius' entourage of nymphs-of-honor.

"Will," said Cleito, "what will happen when we make love?"

Will laughed. "Then others will share our joy. We will have enough privacy not to be embarrassed, my love, don't worry. Absolute privacy is something people will have to learn to give up, it is one of the roots of evil." He pondered. "My dear, I have many things to say to you. Will you forgive me if I sound like a coven-preacher? But I *am* a few years older than you, and I have seen a lot of the world, when I was in different shapes—a Palace page, a minstrel, and more than once a faun, and between times I have been a student here in Siderion—where we have a fine library, I may tell you, which was where I got those stories from, the stories of Old Tellus that I was using to try to charm you with, my sweet, the day we first met at Avonside."

Cleito pressed herself into his arms. "I am more honored, Will, that such a master spy as you should care for a farm wench like me."

"Now you're laughing at me," said Will, laughing himself and kissing her on the lips. "You're no fool, Cleito, but of course you haven't had my opportunities. The whole Western World has been suffering a Dark Age for the last three hundred years—apart from the chronic human darkness—but we hope to end both, and I want to tell you now about our plans, because you are one of us now, and perhaps an important one at that."

"I, important?" said Cleito, surprised. "I can't see how. But go on, my dear. It is a pleasure for me to have *you* as my teacher—just like the first time, Will."

He pressed her hand and led her to the window. The weather was clear, and they seemed to see for an immense distance. Beyond the blue downs that marked the edge of the plain, higher and farther still rose a line of purple mountains showing faintly through the haze of Dextra's thick atmosphere.

"There," said Will, "that purple range is near the frontier. Beyond is the Sabrina valley, and Westria, and the world of ordinary Invader humans. You remember what *that* was like?"

Cleito shuddered. "How could I forget? It's less than a week since I stopped being an Invader myself. Last Friday—exactly seven days ago, good Goddess!—I was in the hands of the Count's torturers."

"Yes," said Will, "and then there was Alvern, and then Ringston. Cleito, my dear, do you realize that what happened to you in Westria was *nothing exceptional*? It was

THE WILDINGS OF WESTRON 137

just typical of human history. I'll take you to our library, and you can sample the classics of Old Tellus for yourself. Rape, slavery, torture, massacre—they're all old human customs. Actually, you got off lightly! There were worse things on Tellus than we've seen in Atlantis, thought I suppose, given time, someone will think of them again. One little example: the Count's punishment for 'treason.' He thought he was inflicting *flaying*—a horrible death. Well, they had that in certain societies of Tellus. In others they had crucifixion, impaling, breaking on the wheel. There was one big island on Tellus—its position was much like our Atlantis, off the west coast of a large continent—a place called Britain. The main kingdom of Britain was England, from which we get our language English, and the basic traditions of our First Landers. England is described in the histories as a most civilized and progressive place. Well, in England for hundreds of years the legal punishment for treason was so horrible that—that I don't want to describe it to you."

"Worse than flaying?" said Cleito, faltering.

"I think so. They dismembered the man while he was still alive, taking care to keep him alive as long as possible. You can read up the filthy details later. Well, that's the sort of thing that humans, ordinary humans, get up to because they do not feel kin with other humans—or other animals. There is a permanent darkness in human flesh. And that's what we of the Wheel are fighting."

"How are you going to fight it?"

"First of all, by conquest," said Will. "We are disputing among ourselves now, but only about the manner and timing of our effort. Sooner or later, the Wheel must turn, as we say—we Wildings must rule Dextra. In Evenor, we have tried to achieve a pattern of what the new society should be like. I think we have succeeded not too badly. How would it be, Cleito, if all Westria—or all Atlantis—were to become like Evenor?"

"Oh, Will, it would be marvelous!" cried Cleito. "But how could it? Even if you did conquer Westron, and changed some of the laws, what then? What of that permanent darkness in human flesh?"

"There is only one thing for it," said Will. "Human flesh must cease."

"What!"

"Yes. Frankly, the human race in its original form is a failure. Even its good impulses are easily corrupted by that inherent darkness, so that idealism very quickly turns into cruelty. Think of those Lord-fearing Akhorians! That's why, my dear, merely *human* revolutions have always been failures. There were people on Tellus who thought somewhat as we do now—they wanted to conquer Old Earth for a new concept of man. They ended up imposing the worst kind of tyranny, using torture just like Lord Basil, massacring thousands of people. That's all hopeless. You see what I mean? We've got to put an *end* to old mankind. Mind you, when the Mothers first allied themselves with Lucius Lee, they were already thinking that. But they allowed themselves to be persuaded otherwise. With Mark and Meriam, my ancestors, they agreed that there should be a balance on Dextra—half native life, half Invader. It didn't work: we got not peace, but the Laser Wars. The only hope for our planet is that all flesh shall become kin—as all flesh is kin here in Evenor."

"Are you going to drive everybody through the Mothers?" said Cleito, startled.

"It will have to come to that, in the long run," said Will. "But of course it will be done gradually, and I hope we won't have to *drive* anybody. First, our friends and sympathizers—people like Ambrose and Myrto and their followers who have remained of Invader flesh for the sake of our cause. Then, other people of good will. As the general population sees that it's not so terrible to be of kin-flesh and eat kin-food, they will come thronging of themselves to be changed over. One only has to make it fashionable. And then one day, perhaps in our own lifetime, all Atlantis will be *kin*. I do devoutly hope it may be so. We must show the human world how it can be done gently and with increase of happiness. If it is not done so, I fear it may be done with great violence and suffering."

"What do you mean?" said Cleito.

"Endor," said Will. "That is a strong country, and a proud one. The Archim—that is, the Supreme Hylist—he is not ready to strike yet, but he is thinking of an overwhelming strike, a once-for-all attack on New Europe. Then there may be another great war, right across the continent, Endor against the whole human world. Endor will win, I think—but the destruction will be terrible. That is why I want to win over Atlantis quickly, and with little bloodshed—to serve as an example, to bring the rest of the world around without a frightful war."

Cleito pondered. "Will, you say everybody must go through the Mothers—everyone of *good will*. But what of the others—the really wicked ones? The Mothers don't change one's inmost being. I can't see Lord Basil turning into a loving person through sympathy, or Count Horold."

"Nor a great many other Swordist lords," agreed Will. "For example, that entire Brunner family. I've known about them, and others like them, for many years, when I was wandering through Westria. No, Cleito, you're quite right. There's only one thing for them: a quick death."

His dark faun eyes flashed fire. Cleito was astonished.

"I never knew you could be so ruthless, Will."

"Mercy to some creatures," said Will, "would be cruelty to others. Not even the Great Mothers could make anything good of Horold or Basil or Norbert—if they were kin-flesh, they would merely infect our souls. When we have got rid of them, then we can begin our real work in Atlantis."

That afternoon, Will showed Cleito around Glass Castle. There were halls, chapels, bedchambers, kitchens—even small laboratories where the odd-looking blue-skinned Gobblers were at work, bending over tubes of glass and coils of wire.

"Among other things," said Will, "the Gobblers are our electricians and experts in physical science. We have no objection to a certain amount of physical science, you know, only we do not rely on it too much. Taken too far, it always leads to death-weapons—or so Porphyry says. You may have noticed that there's no radio mast over Glass Castle."

"Why is that?" asked Cleito. "Is radio a death-weapon?"

Will laughed. "Not at all. But Porphyry and his most adept followers prefer to exercise their *mental* radio. The Assistant Hylists, as we call them—they all have a goodly inheritance of Lee blood—can communicate fairly efficiently without words. There is another consideration, too.

The scientists in the various Agency Temples who control their radios are not all of our party. It would not be safe if they detected radio waves coming from the center of Evenor."

"What's *this* place?" said Cleito.

They were in a translucent tower near the center of the castle; and through an archway of blue bricks they saw a large chamber, wide and high, with tables, chairs, and a great many shelves. There were two blue-skinned Gobblers in the place, one hovering about near the shelves, another sitting at a desk in a corner poring over what seemed to be a small white card. To Cleito's surprise, this latter Gobbler seemed to be wearing a pair of thick-lensed spectacles. As he was otherwise naked, and half covered in thick purple fur, he looked an astonishing figure.

"This is the library," said Will, "and these are Remus and Rasmus, our librarians. Remus is the one with the magnifiers."

As they entered, the two Gobblers left their tasks and came to greet them. Remus had removed the "magnifiers," and now stood blinking at them beside his twin. Like all Gobblers, he had a very broad face, very large nostrils, slit eyes and thin purple lips, a caricature, thought Cleito, of the face of a faun. And yet, she knew, all fauns had been small Gobblers once, before the Great Mothers had speeded up their evolution to conform with human ideas of beauty.

The librarians seemed quite excited to see them. Remus said, in the strange thick Gobbler accent:

"So, my lord, here you are again in the greenie form! Vell, vell, it iss a record, I think—"

"You mean, there iss no record," corrected Rasmus. "No parallel case of vun who vent through so young and then so often."

"That's right," said Remus. "That iss vot I meant. Now, my lord, I hope you vill immediately dictate for us an account of your latest adventures."

"Oh, spare me, you two," said Will laughing. "All right, I'll do it, but not right now—in a few days, all right? And Cleito shall give you her story, too, and then maybe you can make a book of it all."

"That vill be marvelous," said Remus, his narrow eyes

opening to their widest, his goblin-mouth creased in a happy grin. "What shall we call it? The Second Tale of the Turners?"

"The Escapades of Elric," suggested Rasmus. "That is obviously—"

"Why not 'The Wildings of Westron'?" said Will hastily. "You shouldn't give away *too much* in your title, you know."

There was a short silence. Then Remus said: " 'Wildings of Westron' will do very well. We shall start gathering materials immediately. I have in mind first to interview the Lady Bessy for the early history, and then—"

"Remus," said Will, "wouldn't you like to show Cleito all the little marvels of this place now?"

"A pleasure," said Remus. "This vay, please."

For a whole hour Cleito inspected the library. She had never seen so many books in her life, for since printing had been reserved to the Agency, books were great rarities in Atlantis. Luckily, she had been taught to read in coven-school so as to be able to copy out the sabbat service book—a regular chore in the Ring Cult—and now she was able to make at least something of these volumes. Some were priceless treasures: *The Poems of Endymion Lee* (Flora: Centaur Press, 513); *Prolegomena to the Sifted Scriptures*, first edition (Landing City, 482); and even works composed in the fabulous world of Tellus, with dates up to more than 2000 in A.D. reckoning. But these latter were not books in the ordinary sense: they were cards not much bigger than a man's hand, and they had to be read with magnifiers.

"I had thought the old books were all destroyed in the Wars," said Cleito, marveling at a box of cards labeled *English Drama: 1500-1641 A.D.*

"In the left-hand world, the human provinces, they were," said Remus. "But the Archims had the foresight to preserve a library of microcards in Rotaris—and no death-weapons struck Endor. The Legates have brought us copies from time to time, and now we have a complete collection."

"I would like to come here and read some of these," said Cleito, looking at Will. "If we have time, and if they're not too hard for a peasant girl."

"We will have time," said Will.

"And ve vill give you every assistance, my lady," said Rasmus. "In truth, there is much you should know for your future role."

Cleito was puzzled by this remark. After they had thanked the librarians and left the room, she said:

"What is all this, Will? Why does everyone keep calling me 'my lady,' and so forth? What *is* my future role, for Goddess' sake?"

Will laughed. "Glass Castle is a school of courtesy, my dear. Every woman gets called 'lady' here. As for your future role—why, you are going to join the fellowship of the Wheel, are you not? When we all go out to take Westria, you will be one of us, and that will be a serious role, in all conscience."

That evening's feast was doubly joyous in that it was also a feast of the Ring Church: Beltane, the 33rd of April, the Eve of May. The great Glass Hall was seasonably decorated with Wilding hawthorn and yellow tubolia flowers, and every guest wore his gayest clothes. Will and Cleito now had small faun-sized tunics; Cleito had as much steel jewelery as she could bear to wear; and Will wore a small blue cloak decorated with the yellow four-spoked Wheel—for he also, a year previously, had been dubbed a Wheel Knight.

To Cleito's surprise, they were placed at the high table, along with Porphyry, Ferbrand, King Silvius, Melissa, the Gobbler librarians, the Legate Symmachus and a human-centaur named Helenus: a weirdly variegated company. Helenus could not use a normal chair, of course: he had a blocklike stool to support his underbelly and his second set of ribs.

"We think it important," whispered Will, "that every intelligent species should have a representative here. This is not just a festive party, it's also a council of war."

Cleito looked around the hall. The tables were filled with blue-cloaked Knights, gaily dressed ladies—and fauns, Gobblers, and a few centaurs. The servers were both fauns, dressed for the occasion in bright cloths, and human boys and girls, the children of the Knights and their ladies. There were minstrels of several species—all except Gobblers, who had no musical or poetic talents.

Cleito laughed. "A bit of a difference from the Count's feast, Will! And to think, that was just one week ago this night."

The Legate, Symmachus Anders, was a black-haired man of middling height, with bushy black eyebrows. Cleito had heard of his journey, along a regular secret route from Endor down to the Ocean at a small port in Nordica, and thence by sea in a sailing vessel manned by Wheel members to a landing point on the western shore of Evenor. He had come in person with his messages from the Archim Julian because even in the greatest adepts, telepathy was not always reliable.

Symmachus waited till the meal was over, and people of all species were sitting over their glasses of yellow native wine. Then he cleared his throat, looked at Porphyry, and said:

"Shall we use open words now, Hylist?"

Porphyry nodded. "We have no secrets from each other here, my lord Legate. Will you tell the people what has been decreed in Endor?"

"This," said Symmachus loudly and clearly. "Archim Julian and his Council of Adepts have adopted a Four-Year Plan. In four years—in 980—we shall move. In that year, we shall expect you to help—you, and all the other Provincial Hylons, from Nordica to Kataya. One coordinated attack, and we are certain to prevail. Till then, we counsel you to lie low, and increase your armed forces."

"And may I ask," said Porphyry mildly, "from whom you expect the most serious resistance?"

"From the Saints," said Symmachus, "the Livyans, and the Akhorians. They will surely fight to the death, and we will have to invade them from over the sea."

"And supposing," said Porphyry, "that before you launch your great push, the Akhorians conquer Atlantis. Would that not be a grave development?"

"Why, yes," said Symmachus, looking surprised. "But surely they cannot."

Will leaned forward across the table. "Not alone, no. But with a little treachery from within? With a foothold guaranteed to them in our island? Legate, do you realize that Count Horold of Westron is about to sell his people to those pirates?"

Symmachus looked hard at Will, then at Porphyry, but said nothing. Cleito guessed that a conversation was proceeding, but on a plane where she could not follow it.

"I see," said the Legate at last. "You want to launch a forestalling attack. So long as no word gets abroad, in the left-hand world, about Endor, I can see no objection in principle. But in the circumstances of Westria today, surely it is perilous? That laser—"

Porphyry smiled almost ferociously. "That laser is going to fight on *our* side. Already it is destroying the Count."

"Oh yes?" said Symmachus. "How?"

"Imagine," said Porphyry, addressing the hall at large. "Here is this one man with this one deadly weapon. He is an absolute tyrant, but there is nobody he can really trust. Even in his own family, whom do you think he can give the laser to, and be sure it will not be used on himself? His sons? Every one of them hates him, both the bastards and the legitimate princes, and would like to see him dead. The Lord Basil? I think not. So, what does Horold do *when he goes to sleep?*"

"He puts the laser under his pillow," said Ferbrand.

"Right. But that does not give him a restful night! And I rather think it will be spoiling his pleasure with his favorite concubines."

There was a roar of laughter from all the guests. Cleito, imagining the scene in the Count's great bedchamber, laughed as loud as anyone.

"As things are," said Porphyry, "what with our contacts in Westron, it would not be difficult for us to get Horold assassinated. But that would not serve our purposes. In his place there would come a worse Count—probably Basil, who is equally pro-Akhorian. No, it must be open war, and that quickly, before the Akhorians are too strong in Westria—preferably this year, before Midsummer. Our army is not as big as the Count's, but I think it is more deadly—"

"Apart from that laser," said Symmachus.

"Apart from that," agreed Porphyry. "But there is a limit to what he can do with that popgun, as he will find.

We can field a thousand mounted Knights, and three thousand human infantry—"

"And a thousand Myrmies," broke in the centaur Helenus, with a savage grin. "Riderless Myrmies, My lord Legate! The Count's army have never faced those—I doubt if they will face them for long. Even if they stand their charge, Myrmies have one great advantage in battle: they are not dismayed by losses! Kill nine hundred and ninety-nine, and the thousandth will still come at you as fiercely as ever, with hoofs and claws."

Symmachus laughed. "I know—we have some in Endor, too."

"And we have another weapon," said Porphyry, looking at Will. "Disaffection in Westria. The Navy especially hates the Akhorians, and the common people have no love for their present Count. Of course, we have no great liking for these little autocracies, but if it is expedient, we could set up a Count of our own for Westria—even a King of Atlantis, one of ourselves who is yet a legitimate Prince, by the custom of two centuries."

Symmachus shrugged. "Very well: I make no objection. Yes, a Wheel Knight King of Atlantis could be useful to our cause. But I am thinking that when your Midsummer Day dawns, he had better be in a more impressive shape than at present. The Westrians will not rally to a faun!"

At that moment there came a disturbance in the body of the hall. Some people had just entered at the main door, an old Wilding Knight and his elderly lady. This gray-haired woman now came rushing up to the high table and fell on her knees just in front of Will, reaching out her arms to him. She was in tears—tears of mingled joy and sorrow.

"My boy—my little Elric—is it really you, child?" she cried. "They told me you would be so, and I don't care as long as you are safe again. Oh, don't do it any more, Elric William! Never again, if you love your old nurse!"

"Well, I won't, Bessy," said Will gently. "Get up, get up, please. You and Uncle Richard—we'll find you places here at our table."

Cleito had risen, and she was staring hard at the old woman, Lady Bessy.

"Darling," said Will, "Uncle Richard and Bessy are the

nearest thing to a family that I have in the world. They have a country house on the north edge of Siderion—and that's where I was brought up, from the age of two."

Then Cleito, in her turn, sank to her knees before her lover. O Goddess, she thought, what a fool I have been. I should have guessed.

Aloud, she said: "My Prince, am I the lass whom the true Count will love?"

"Yes, my Countess," said Will, and leaned forward and kissed her on the forehead, just under her blue nymph's hair.

And all the people of Siderion shouted for joy.

Chapter
THIRTEEN

The next morning Porphyry summoned Will and Cleito to his cell-like quarters in the heart of the Glass Castle, and laid strict injunctions upon them.

"Prince Elric William," he said, "you and your lady are hereby ordered to take a holiday. We are not going to move until you can safely be changed, Will—not for three or four weeks at least—and you both badly need a rest after your travels and tribulations. So long as you do not stray too far from Siderion, you may go where you like. Your room will be kept for you here, but you might also like to visit Silvania—King Silvius is eager to entertain you there—and then there is Ferrol."

"I would like first to take Cleito to Cleve," said Will.

Cleve was the country home of old Sir Richard Lee and his wife Bessy, Will's foster parents; the home also of Ferbrand, whom Cleito had now discovered to be Richard's son, and therefore Will's elder foster brother. She had heard the whole story: how Bessy Newston, the court lady of Westron, had taken refuge with two-year-old Will in the Agency on that terrible day nineteen years ago when the Trinovantian conquerors had burst into the city; how Ambrose had passed them both through the Mother in the courtyard; and how, as a faun-woman and her child, they had been led by agents of the Wheel to Evenor and restored to human form by the Great Mothers. Also how the Lady Bessy had married the widower knight Sir Richard, and how Will had grown up at Cleve, on the northern edge of Siderion, like any other Wilding boy—yet always reminded by Bessy of his princely blood and heritage.

"Why didn't you tell me at once, Will?" said Cleito when she had heard the whole history. "My dear liege lord—"

"That's why," said Will. "Here, none of this 'liege lord' stuff, Cleity! It's all nonsense, anyway. It's only an accident of history that some character with the surname Turner made himself autocrat of Westron in the darkest of the Dark Centuries, and declared Westria County 'free' of the rest of Atlantis. We want to *reverse* all that. It's true my poor family in the last few generations were not bad Counts as Counts go; also that I'm to be Count again if we win. But in the end, Counts and Kings are going to be dumped, and a good thing too! I am proud to be a Wheel Knight, Cleity—nothing more."

But Cleito, as they rode through Siderion that fine Mayday morning, could not help being proud of her princely lover, the young faun who was also a Knight of the Wheel and a Count of Atlantis; she knew that since his boyhood Will had been concerned with his destiny in and responsibility for Westria, and she was acutely conscious of what she considered her own unworthiness—she, a farm girl—to be even temporarily Countess of Westron.

There were just five of them who rode together that day—old Sir Richard, Bessy, Ferbrand, Will and Cleito. Before they left the Glass Castle, Melissa had said shyly:

"If ye forbid me not, Cleity, I shall remain awhile with King Silvius' people. I would know more of the great faun-folk, the golden ones. And my lord the King expects you and Will to visit him in Silvania presently, so in a week or two we shall see each other again."

And thus Melissa and Cleito had kissed and parted.

Cleve was a single-story mansion of yellow brick set in a park of blue beech trees just coming into leaf under a blue grassy down.

"We are quite close to Ferrol here," said Will, as they dismounted from their Myrmies near the front door. "In fact, it's just over the hill. The Gobblers are our near neighbors. They built this house, they provide us with pagegirls—"

"Page*girls*!" exclaimed Cleito. "I never heard of *that* before."

"Well, maid forsterlings, or whatever you like to call them," said Will. "One of the master smiths of Ferrol has sent us his twin daughters to be trained up in civility—and to help about the house. Ah, here they are, Cundry and Caris."

Cleito was amused to see two solemn-looking Gobbler girls, their blue skins largely hidden by neat white tunics. Cundry and Caris greeted Will with joy.

"Ve vere most afraid for you, fair Sir Villiam," said Cundry.

"But it is good to see you again, Master Will," said Caris, her slit eyes gleaming. "And so much more handsome than before! Vhy, in that shape you are almost as beautiful as a Goblin boy."

And everybody laughed.

"Oh, Will, it is good to be here!" said Cleito, taking her lover's hand. "I—I have no family of my own, but—"

"But now you *do* have one," said Will, kissing her. "Yes, it is good to get home."

They stayed at Cleve for a week, a week full of simple happiness, and then, guided by Cundry, Will and Cleito spent another week exploring the industrial valley of Ferrol. Cleito was amazed by the things she saw there—foundries and workshops, and iron almost as plentiful as aluminum. At present the smiths of Ferrol were hard at work turning out steel swords and daggers and spearpoints for the coming war; but Cundry's father found time to show the travelers the most delicate pieces of Gobbler art, including lovely steel brooches and jewelry.

"I had thought," said Cleito, as they rode back to Cleve, "that Evenor was a mere wilderness. Now I know better."

"A mere wilderness is no place for men," said Will, "not even for Wilding men. Silvania, now—that's wild indeed; but that's for fauns and Gods, and it suits them. I hope one day there will be more Ferrols in the world. We must return Dextra to the good days before the seventh century—and then go on from there to better things still."

At Cleve they found that Ferbrand had ridden back to the Glass Castle, and they now followed him: but at the capital of Evenor there was still no news from Westria, and nothing dramatic to do. Will spent several days there holding discussions with his brother Knights and Porphyry—the legate Symmachus had returned to Endor. Cleito used this time to read some essential books in the library, mostly histories of Dextra. Rasmus and Remus tried to restrain themselves while she was pursuing this necessary course of self-education, but sometimes the temptation was too strong for them, and Cleito found herself narrating her adventures to the purple-furred librarians, who took notes avidly.

"Ven ve write this up," said Remus, his eyes gleaming, "ve shall avail ourselves of the ancient privileges of historians; from vot you have said, Lady Cleito, ve can even reconstruct your thoughts—as human, as faun—"

"It's going to be a crazy book, then!" laughed Cleito.

Finally, they visited Silvania. This was the country west of the valley of Siderion, and it was nearly all purple woods, blue glades, and cold clean streams. The people were mostly green fauns, with just a sprinkling of goldskins like the King. The greenes only occasionally had bothered to make themselves dwellings—little huts of boughs or even the interiors of hollow trees. For the most part they lived wild, and slept in nests of blue grass under the sky. But the goldskins had built themselves—or had got the greenies to build them—some very neat houses of light tubolia stems and faded blue thatch. At least, Cleito thought of these buildings as "houses"—they were about the size of Westrian cottages—but the goldskins invariably called them palaces. Cleito soon realized that the goldskins were rather vain, in a somewhat endearing fashion. They had adopted high-sounding names, such as Polymnia and Atalanta and Astarte for the golden girls, and Aristaeus, Palinurus and Theagenes for the boys. The green fauns seemed to hold the goldskins in great awe and love.

King Silvius entertained them at a simple feast, at which however the wild wine flowed in abundance. Silvius soon relaxed his rather formidable dignity; he was especially kind to his maid-of-honor Melissa, allowing her to sit at his feet and fill his wine cup—and to gaze at him adoringly.

That night Will and Cleito shared a nook of the tubolia-wood "palace," a place sufficiently private with light wooden screens. Cleito whispered:

"Will, did you notice—about Melissa, I mean?"

"I could even feel it," said Will, laughing softly. "She is very far gone, poor girl. I did not think fauns could feel so *seriously*."

"Will, what nonsense! we're fauns ourselves."

"Not quite. You ought to know the difference, my dear. You were pure nymph for a couple of days."

Cleito gave a little shudder. "Yes. But I suppose Melissa has had more practice. She's always had a *personality*, which is more than I had. So I suppose it's not impossible that she should fall in love with Silvius. Poor thing, she can't possibly have any chance there. He might make love to her, of course—it's physically possible, isn't it? But anything more—there's just no way."

"But there *is* a way," said Will suddenly. "The Mothers!"

"What?"

"The Great Mothers. Their forest is only a few hours' journey south of here. Cleito, don't forget that the Great Mothers are *intelligent*. A person can talk to them, ask to be altered in a certain way. What do you say we go to them tomorrow, with Melissa—and ask them to make her a goldskin?"

"Good Goddess!" cried Cleito. "Would they? And would she be the same person?"

"Well—she might seem a little *prouder*," said Will. "At least for the first few days. But she ought to come to herself afterward—just as you did. And *then*—Silvius likes her already. Why shouldn't he? You know the goldies have permanent mates for the most part—but Silvius so far has no queen."

"Queen Melissa!" said Cleito. "No, *Goddess* Melissa! Holy Rings! But why not?"

But next morning Melissa did not want to leave the palace of King Silvius. As they walked together in a nearby grove of tetron trees, she said, faintly blushing:

"I thank you, Will and Cleito, for your kind wishes, and the honor ye would do me. But I know not as yet if he would like it. By his great favor, I am permitted to be his maid here for a while. If ye would come back to Silvania in a week, or ten days, then perhaps..."

"All right," said Will, smiling. "Now here is a nice thing, Melissa: at last I have met a true faun-girl who is *shy*."

When they had said goodbye to Silvius and Melissa, Will said:

"Perhaps it is best so. I have a slight uneasy feeling. Even though I am no Adept, but at the best of times merely a simple Knight, there are so many powerful minds in Evenor that one can't help picking up warnings. I think we should return to Siderion before we go to the Mothers. Could it be that there is some messenger approaching at last, from Westron?"

It could. When Will and Cleito got back to the Glass Castle, they were met by Ferbrand at the outer gate. His green eyes looked grave.

"Myrto has arrived," he said. "Will you both go to the Great Hall at once?"

In the hall, Porphyry sat enthroned with a hundred Adepts and Wheel Knights in their stalls behind and on either side of him, as well as a few centaurs couched close by on their blocklike stools. Facing this assembly were a little group of humans, men and women in travel-stained tunics or jerkins such as one might see any day in the villages or on the roads of Westria. But their leader was a stately woman with beautiful long black hair like a cascade of night.

For a month now Cleito had not come into contact with ordinary humans of Invader flesh. Now, she mentally recoiled. Myrto's being she could faintly perceive—the priestess' telepathic faculty was strong enough to leap the "wall between left and right"—but the others were like walking statues, mere simulacra of humanity. She remembered her first moments of life as "Chloe," and how dead and hollow the men of the Agency had seemed. The effect now was quite similar. The permanent darkness of original human flesh stood embodied before her. She was glad she was not close enough to *smell* them. And yet these were good people, friends....

The party from Westria had been given stools to sit on,

but now Myrto rose, looked all about her at the assembled members of the Wheel and spoke.

"Blessed be," she said in her sweet clear voice. "My friends, I rejoice to see you in the flesh at last, and this wonderful place in which we used to believe only through faith and mental contact. But it is a dire occasion which brings me, as some of you already know."

"Myrto, my sister," said Porphyry, "you had better repeat your news. We are not all Adepts here—and these tidings should be to all the leaders of our army."

"Very well," said Myrto. "hear then, all of you . . ."

From the priestess' very first words, Cleito felt a sense of shock. Westria, dear familiar Westria, had become a place of darkness, of persecution, and of something very like a foreign invasion. Briefly, the events of the past four weeks were as follows:

The Agency radio in Westron had transmitted to all the other Agency establishments of the world the news that Count Horold possessed a laser gun and refused to surrender it. At once various states of Atlantis had begun to make threatening noises—those which followed the Ring Cult talked of a "cyclade" or Holy War on behalf of the Agency and the Covenant. Horold had countered by inviting the envoys of Vitrin, Suthron, Camlan, Amaurot and Trinovant to a demonstration: he had lined up some petty criminals, dressed for the occasion in complete armor, and had cut their living bodies in two with a single sweep of his gun.

This had silenced most of the other Free Counties at once; but the Governor of Trinovant, Horold's hostile elder brother Havion, had persisted. He had sent a herald to Westron, demanding with all protocol a "battle of a hundred knights"—a formal tourney, of which the prize would be the laser or final recognition by Trinovant of Westria's independence. Horold of course had refused, in serious interstate quarrels in Atlantis, tourneys were normally proposed by one side and turned down by the other as a prelude to "informal" battle—that is, total war. Trinovant seemed about to march, but then a squadron of the High Emir's navy was seen off the mouth of the Isis, the river of Trinovant. . . .

And at home, Horold had struck. He had come to realize that Ambrose, the Chief Agent, was an enemy. First he had put forward a candidate for Agency training in Biology—his own son by a concubine, a young man of eighteen years named Harxen. Ambrose, playing for time, had accepted Harxen as a novice; he had no alternative, since the youth had the right qualifications—he could read, and he was interested in hunting and falconry. Harxen was also obviously interested in spying for his father, but Ambrose had kept him out of the Courtyard of Flaying for a couple of weeks.

The crisis had come with the case of the unfortunate stock-trader John Mack. After being tortured for weeks in Westgate prison, Mack had been condemned to death, and the Count, prompted by Basil, had demanded that Mack be flayed by Ambrose *in the presence of the novice Harxen*.

Ambrose had refused. Flaying was a delicate operation, only Biologists who had passed through a year's training could attend.

Horold had replied, "My son is an outstanding candidate. In his case, two weeks are as good as a year. They had better be. Otherwise, I shall become a Biologist myself, in half a day."

Ambrose had immediately barricaded himself in the Agency, reporting developments to the outside world by radio, and awaiting attack.

It had come, but not in the form he had expected. Not a direct assault by the Count's troops—which might indeed have provoked a "cyclade"—but an internal attempted coup.

"Some of the Physicists," said Myrto, "banded together with Harxen and tried to burst into the Biology courtyards. This is utterly contrary to Agency discipline, of course—the Sciences are strictly separated, in order to prevent dangerous Progress—but this move would not have violated the international Covenant. Anyway, Goddess be thanked, the move failed. Ambrose gave the mind-word to the Warrior Mother, and she turned on her defensive mental field. In a few seconds, the Physicists and Harxen were reduced to idiocy, they fled out of the Agency altogether, raving!

"Horold was furious, of course. He suspected now that

there was something gravely wrong with the process that Ambrose called 'flaying.' So he took poor Mack, and had him simply beheaded. His family he enslaved. Yes, *enslaved!* The Count has issued a decree making slavery legal in Westria—minor criminals will be made slaves, with exactly the same status as fauns.

"This should please Horold's new allies. The young Emir Barak has not returned, and there is a squadron of his ships in the Sabrina, just below Westron.

"Finally, there is our own story. As soon as Barak appeared, the Count decreed that Swordism-Lordism was the only legal religion of Westria. And he sent Basil and his squads to arrest me and the other principal coven leaders. But of course we had warning—faun to faun, you know—and so we were already on our way to Evenor. Thanks to you, my lord Hylist, we knew the mind-word to pass the Warrior Mothers unharmed—and so, here we are."

"Well," said Porphyry, as Myrto resumed her stool, "thank you, dear sister. You and your companions will be hungry presently, I think, but we have the remedy for that ill not too far away: the Great Mothers. And now," he continued, turning to his Knights, "what think you, my people, that we should do?"

Will stepped forward into the middle of the Hall. "Fight!" he called, in a voice which carried to every corner of the great chamber. "We cannot wait another day. In my wanderings through Westria I saw the evils of the Count's men increasing, the disease gathering to eat away the life of my poor country. Now the foulness is ripe to bursting, and the time is ripe too for us to destroy it. My brothers, fellow Knights of the Wheel, I call for war—instant, open war."

At once the hall re-echoed with the shouts of the Knights. In a hundred voices the one word rang out—"War!"

Porphyry smiled grimly. "That cry will be heard far," he said. "In every household of Westria where there are fauns, our little friends will be stirring. Well, the voice of the people . . . But there is one thing, Prince Elric William: I am no warrior. We need a general for our forces."

Ferbrand strode forward. "Fellow Knights," he said, "there is only one leader we can logically elect for this enterprise. When he was in his own shape and strength, you all know how my foster brother was a most valiant Knight, accomplished at weaponplay and well able to conduct a squadron. I propose that in this war against the usurper Horold, we follow the true Count of Westron, our friend and brother Elric William, who—"

The rest of his speech was lost in a roar of approbation from the whole assembly. Porphyry rose, smiling, from his throne.

"Well, Will, you see that you are elected our Warlord. But this is no office for a little green faun. Another time is ripe, now. Tomorrow many of us shall journey into the forest called Matrum."

West of Siderion, south of Silvania, the purple land dips to a wide valley sloping steadily to the south. There are hills on the east of this area, and also on the west. This sheltered, south-sloping plain is the warmest part of Evenor: under the thick-growing Mandrakes and tentrons, the air is almost steamy, like a New Asian jungle. But this great brooding forest is intersected with wide trails, avenues which look as though they have been cut by man; though in truth they have not.

The wide trails themselves intersect, and at the places where they meet are ample clearings. In each clearing there abides a being which can equally well be described as a plant, or as an animal. Like an animal, the Mother can move when necessary, but normally she prefers not to—she anchors herself in the hollow she had excavated in the center of her clearing, turning her millipede legs into rootlets. And there she lives through years and centuries, not so much an individual as a cell in a mighty brain, whose other cells extend through other forests—some in Endor, some in Anthis, some in Hind, indeed, all across the land surface in the warmer and wetter regions of Dextra.

There are some men and other beings who can converse with the Great Mothers to some extent at any time, by reason of their own unusual mental powers. But lesser mortals are able to do this only if they eat of a certain product of a Mother's body—a round disclike cake which grows on the ends of the leaf-bearing arms. And thus it was that on a morning of early summer, in a clearing of the Matrum forest, a great many people were gathered, and some few of these were going forward, preparing to eat the plant-cakes.

Prophyry the Hylist was there, officiating as priest and president of the ceremonies, and around the edges of the clearing stood Ferbrand and a dozen other Wheel Knights, Sir Richard and Lady Bessy, and King Silvius of Silvania. Myrto and her companions were not there, for they had gone to other Mothers in nearby clearings; but close to the great Plant, side by side, knelt three naked green fauns—Melissa, Will and Cleito.

In her heart, Cleito was filled with solemn exultation, but also sadness. The previous night, she and Will had made love once more in faun fashion. Once more they had merged in that fiery ring of body and mind—and had known that it was for the last time. From now on, if the Mother accomplished the wished-for transformation, they would be restored to human shape in right good Wilding flesh—and would be deprived of that enormous physical ecstasy. O Goddess, prayed Cleito, thanks. Thanks, that I have known that, and Will has known that in me, and known me so. But I know also that all things must end—even I myself one day—and good things are not abolished because they are passed in time. The Ring must turn. So be it.

Then, together, they all three ate of the plant-cakes.

Cleito was aware, gradually, of a vast humming, and a sweet scent. And then there came a voice through the humming that was not a voice borne through the air or heard with ears of flesh.

—Greetings, little movers, good kin-substance children! One of you is known to us of old, Elric-Rondel-Wender-Will. We perceive your thought and your desire, and we shall mold you even as you wish: once more. Once more only can this be done to you, else . . . else your time of disintegration will arrive, which we do not wish, since your inmost structure should have usefulness for many revolutions more.

—But there are also you others. What does the little

mover Melissa require of us? ... That? ... There is no difficulty. Melissa is a healthy young one, and the transformation will be even less in bulk than in the case of Elric. Melissa and Elric, you should lay yourselves in two several petals, and in a quarter of a day you will be even as you wish.

Thank you, Mother of fauns, said Melissa excitedly in the mind-speech. O thank you forever!

—But what would you other three wish? said the humming voice.

What—what other three? asked Cleito mentally. There is only myself in this place who wishes also to be changed.

—How can you be so ignorant of your own being! In that body which you call your *self* there are three, two very little within the big third. Is it only the big one that calls itself Cleito-Chloe?

Cleito was seized with amazement. But even in her ethereally drugged condition she remembered one Dextran fact of life: that nymphs do not menstruate, and so have to depend on inner awareness for certain early warnings. And her own inner condition, being always unusual, abnormal even for a nymph, had failed to supply her with any such warning. She now mentally asked for clarification, and received it.

—Yes: two small females, already of five weeks. They will be pure she she-fauns, on every level of being.

O Great Mother, said Cleito, can I be changed now like Will—into the kin-human form?

—*You* can be changed, containing one; but those which you contain will disintegrate. After about one week the spore is developing too fast—and the change remains too dangerous until one year after the birth.

O Goddess, no! cried Cleito.

Will spoke mentally: You can still go through, Cleito. I would not blame you. We may have other children. As for me—I *have* to go through now.

Cleito was torn with anguish. A nymph's gestation period is nearly as long as a human female's. For some seven months at least, she would be separated from Will by a difference of *species*. He a warrior, a man, a prince, a hero—and she a little green faun-girl. A pregnant nymph.

THE WILDINGS OF WESTRON 159

But after, she said to the Mother, when the little ones are more than one year old—can they be changed to humans? Kin-humans?

—Yes: that will be safe. But they will always be a little different from humans in their inmost being. The most important areas of the brain will always retain a trace—just as you retain a trace of your humanity even in nymph form, Cleito-Chloe. That is unalterable now.

Two little daughters who are really nymphs in human form, thought Cleito—and her thinking was also a saying, since in this mode of being there was no difference, no privacy of thought whatever.

She felt the love radiating from Will. It was love for her, Cleito—but also for two little nymph daughters who hardly yet existed, and now might never exist. And then Cleito knew her duty.

You must be a man, Will, she thought-said, but I must remain a nymph—until I have borne these little creatures.

At least, she added, bearing them won't hurt a bit!

Six hours later, as the declining invisible sun filled all the world with dim golden light, the shimmering globes burst, the boat-sized petals shriveled and rolled down, and two naked forms were revealed to the onlookers. Silvius uttered a great cry of joy.

"Queen Melisande!" he said.

It was indeed a beautiful, tall, gold-skinned, green-haired girl who stirred on the dry bed of her petal, and smiled up at her golden King in rapturous gratitude and love. Melissa-Melisande was as tall as Cleito had been when she was in human form; now, since Cleito was not in human form, she looked the more human of the two, with her stately features and rounded ears.

But Cleito was not looking at Melissa now.

The other figure disclosed by a burst petal was that of a naked young man, brown-eyed, brown-haired, with a lightly tanned skin. He was as beautiful in his manly way as Melissa in her womanly one; and his face was the face of Will the Minstrel. But his eyes did not open.

Cleito flung herself upon the body.

"Will! Oh, Will—" she cried, racked with fear.

Porphyry stepped forward. "Calm yourself, Lady Cleito," he said. "There is one faculty of kin-flesh—a mournful one, perhaps. If your lover does die, you will know of it at once, in your heart."

And then the young man's eyes fluttered, and the lids came slowly apart. He managed a tired smile.

"Cleity," he said, "you are the prettiest nymph I have ever seen; and also the best woman in the world, my Countess."

Chapter
FOURTEEN

In the upper valley of the Sabrina River, the 6th of June, 976, dawned clear after a night of gentle rain. It was a Monday, the weekday of the First Landing, and hence the sabbat or sabbath for all the religions of Dextra. That early morning the good people of Arlow-on-Sabrina were making certain preparations, when they looked out of their front windows and were startled to see strange riders occupying their Market Square.

Arlow is a small market town on the west bank of the Sabrina some fifty kilometers upstream from Westron, at a place where a ferry crosses the river and a road runs eastward out of Westria to Trinovant. The people of the place were devout followers of the Ring Church. Now that the Count had proscribed their sect and closed the Arlow covenstead, they had made stealthy arrangements to hold that morning's sabbat in the nearby purple woods. Therefore, with the weight of their guilt upon them, they were frightened almost to death when they first caught sight, in the early dawn, of a hundred or so Knights in blue cloaks bearing strange banners and mounted on even stranger steeds.

"May it be the Count's new outlandish allies?" said the Mayor's wife fearfully to her husband. Their house fronted directly on the square, only fifty meters from the central Ring monument. "That Emir Barak—they say he is for putting down the worship of the good Goddess with a strong hand."

"The Akhorians wear green tunics, not blue cloaks,"

said the Mayor, staring through a chink in his front curtains. "And—for Goddess' sake! What kind of hexips are *those*?"

The faun servants had silently appeared in the parlor. The Mayor's old faun butler said:

"Fear not, good Maister—these be not Akhorians, they be the soldiers of the True Count of Westron. See, they are rising his standard."

In fact, there were two standards now flying over the Ring monument. One was blue, with a golden four-spoked Wheel as its central device; the other was a red-and-white flag, bearing a red Ring on a white ground. The Mayor had never seen the first before, but he was old enough to remember the second.

"The Turner Counts!" he breathed—and rushed out of his house. Once in the square, he was in time to hear the herald's echoing proclamations:

"... Our High and Mighty Prince, and Liege Lord, Count Elric the Fourth, by the Grace of the Goddess, Sovereign Prince of this Free County of Westria. Goddess Save the Count!"

Beside the standards on the steps of the market monument stood a young man with brown hair, dressed in a surcoat of the House of Turner and a blue cloak. He had raised his fine steel sword, and with this he was giving the ritual salute and challenge to the four quarters of the world that is given by every sovereign of Atlantis when he assumes his title. Around the steps he marched and raised the sword hilt to his lips facing toward the east, the south, the west, and the north.

And now the people of Arlow were flocking to him, forgetting their fear of the strange centaur-steeds. The Mayor pressed forward, eager to be the first to render homage, as befitted his rank and office. But the humans had been anticipated by dozens of faun servants, and foremost of all there knelt before Count Elric a green-skinned nymph girl, barefoot like all fauns but otherwise dressed in a small tunic and over-robe like any human Westrian lady.

The young Count took her hands in his and kissed her on her green forehead, and all the people could see that there were tears in his eyes.

"In you, Lady Cleito," he said, "I accept the homage of

all Westria, both of my loyal fauns and my loyal humans; and may they be equal friends and companions from henceforth."

At last the Mayor got his chance to kneel.

"My Prince," he cried, "can it really be you? Everyone believed you were dead."

Will smiled. "I will soon convince them otherwise," he said.

Immediately after the ceremony, Will led Cleito aside to where Ferbrand was standing with a dozen Knights and their Myrmie mounts.

"Ferbrand," said Will, "I would now have you escort my lady twenty kilometers west, to a place within the line of Warrior Mothers in Evenor. You know the spot we choose."

"Oh, Will!" protested Cleito.

"My dear, there is nothing you can do here now to aid us—and we may be fighting within hours. I want you safe at all cost. Ferbrand—"

"Will, *can't* I travel with your army? Nymphs aren't really in much danger from anybody, they get ignored."

"What we just did," said Will, "was not done in a corner. Messengers and spies know that there is one very special nymph, one very dear to the Pretender Elric, and then—"

"Young woman," broke in Ferbrand, "don't argue with our general! This is war, and he just gave you an order."

Cleito submitted. "Oh, Will," she said, "if only you know how hard it is sometimes to be—just a female—"

Will kissed her. "But I do know, my dear: I can still feel your feeling, we are both kin-flesh. Yes, it is hard for you, worse than for me. But you are also serving, my little warrior. You serve us best by being perfectly safe. Try not to worry too much. If things go badly, you will know at once. But there is good reason to hope they will go well."

A few minutes after Cleito and Ferbrand had departed, a curious incident occurred in the marketplace of Arlow. More squadrons of Knights and many troops of Wilding footsoldiers had now entered the town, and Will was marshaling his brigade in preparation for an advance southward down the Sabrina. There were quite a few fauns and country people hanging around the edges of the square, marveling at the strange soldiers and their Myrmies.

And then suddenly there was a small boy in the middle of the square. He might have been an ordinary peasant boy of Westria—he was barefoot and wore a colorless short smock—but his mop of untidy hair was blue, not a deep uniform blue like the natural hair of fauns, but a dirty streaky blue, as though the boy's hair had been dyed, and dyed not too well.

The lad knelt in the square before Will. He was about ten or eleven years old. Behind him now was a knot of humans—apparently a prosperous burgess of the town and his wife and elder children.

"Please, Your Highness," said the boy with the blue hair, "please, now that you're the new Count, is it the law still that I should be a slave?"

The burgess too bent his knee before Will. "Your Highness, we're quite willing to free young Tom. He's a good boy, and we've been doing our best for him, poor lad. But—can we have our money back? I had to pay six pieces in the stock market in Westron when they sold him and his family."

"Slavery is no longer legal in Westria," said Will coldly. "As for your money, man, you will be repaid if I think you deserve it. But come now—the whole story."

In a few minutes, he had heard it. The boy was Tom Mack. He and his mother and young sister had been sold like cattle, or like fauns, in the main marketplace of Westron, auctioned off by agents of Count Horold. Like fauns they had been exposed for sale naked, and to mark them as chattels, their hair had been dyed a more or less faun-like blue.

Tom Mack had no complaints against the burgess who had bought him—the Arlovian had treated him as well as he had dared, indeed more like an apprentice than a slave.

"But," said the boy tearfully, "my—my mother—"

His mother and sister had been sold to the Brunners of Alvern.

Will comforted the lad as best he could. "We shall march to Alvern as soon as we can," he said.

THE WILDINGS OF WESTRON

The news of the proclamation at Arlow had indeed traveled like a flash of lightning—or at least, as fast as a boat could speed down the Sabrina to Westron. In one particular boat was a trader who had had many dealings in the past with Lord Basil. And he had been given an official document to convey to "Horold Harkness, pretended Count of Westron"—a challenge in the usual form to do battle, with a hundred Knights on each side, against Elric IV for the throne of Westria: a challenge certain to be refused, and really equivalent to a declaration of war.

By midday of June 6th, Count Horold, in his Palace presence chamber, had taken this document from the hand of his First Chamberlain, the faun Nemon, and was reading it with incredulity.

"Maniacs, jesters," he snarled, "there are no such Knights, and no such Prince!"

But over the next few hours, report after report confirmed the first news from Arlow. There were more than a hundred blue-cloaked Knights in the upper Sabrina valley, a whole army had emerged from the purple forests of Evenor, an army which used monstrous, savage centauroids instead of hexips as cavalry animals. All of Westria north of Arlow was in their hands—without a fight, the towns and villages of the upper valley had all pledged their allegiance to Elric IV. And the incredible invaders were marching south, toward the capital.

"They shall be fought with, then," roared the Count. "Nemon, I shall leave *you* in charge of Westron, and take Narses with me. There is really no *man* I can trust."

On June 8th, Horold's advance guards made contact with some blue-cloaked Knights and two sorts of centaurs near Mandrake End, a village halfway between Westron and Arlow. There was a brief skirmish—it lasted not much more than five minutes. Horold's knights, led by Sir Hugo Brunner of Alvern, suddenly found themselves being charged by riderless centaurs who nevertheless moved with the concerted weight and precision of highly trained cavalry. Sir Hugo himself was assailed by a blue-furred centaur who first broke lances with him, then flung a blockwood club at his belly, then belabored him over the head with a metal mace, and finally grappled, tearing out his throat with powerful clawed fingers. When Hugo fell, his followers broke and fled back to the main army.

The next reconnaissance was led by Lord Basil and Norbert Brunner, the new Baron of Alvern. They found no enemy at Mandrake End: the blue-cloaked Knights and the monstrous centaurs had withdrawn westward, and were drawn up in battle array on the edge of the Evenor hills.

Count Horold smiled when he heard this. "We will drive these outlaws back into the great forest," he said, patting the holster at his belt. "Once let *me* get at them, and no overgrown senties will stand before us."

By the afternoon of the 10th, the main armies were facing each other. Count Horold rode along his line looking westward; he was accompanied by Lord Basil, the Princes Steelmon and Ferizel, and the Chamberlain Narses. The enemy was hardly visible at all, except as a banner here and there among the purple trees.

"I don't like it," growled Basil. "By my advice, Lord Count, my brother, you will not give battle this evening. Let us wait till dawn—then we will have the light behind us. It is already dark under those trees."

The Count reined in his hexip with an impatient tug. The common soldiers who stood nearby reported afterward that he looked weary; his mouth twitched.

"Basil, you have not the courage of a true-born gentleman," he said. "If it is dark, I will make it light enough for you." He turned and waved to the mounted knights of his bodyguard.

"Draw your swords," he shouted, "and follow me!"

Then he rode straight at the trees in the enemy's center, and drew his gun, and pressed the lever.

Trees began toppling, tetrons cut asunder at a meter above ground fell with a resounding crash. There were few animal cries in the undergrowth—obviously, the first line of the enemy consisted of centaurs. The Count chuckled, and continued waving his deadly tube. But it is not easy to abolish a forest; there is too much falling debris. It took a minute or two of steady firing before there was a clear hole in the center of the treeline, and into this at last the Westrian Knights charged.

For a hundred meters or so they met no opposition: the

enemy center seemed to have been wiped out, or to have melted away. The Count checked his hexip, wheeling to one side in the rear of his knights.

"Roll up their line!" he roared. "Son Steelmon, give the order through—"

The knights were already turning. But what was this? They were not riding to right and left, but straight back toward their own army—and at full gallop! They passed the Count like madmen, screaming, their weapons cast aside. Even their hexips seemed crazed, rolling their eyes, baring their teeth, grinning horribly.

Those knights did not stop their dreadful rout until they were trampling the tents of the Count's infantry. Then the whisper flew around the army—the Madness had struck again; the Count's bodyguard were in as bad a state as the Physicists of the Agency . . . and now what could ordinary soldiers do against witchcraft and Agency magic?

That night the entire army fled. Luckily for the Count, he had reinforcements coming up, led by the Swordist barons of southern Westria; and these checked the rout at the village of Mandrake End.

By the evening of the 11th, the Count and his sons had once more organized a camp. This time the Count listened to Basil's advice, and pitched the tents on an open hill of green grass, well clear of the nearest cover—a streambed to the west, half shrouded with Giant Mandrake trees.

And certain followers of Norbert Brunner were whispering through the army that Lord Basil would make a better leader and a better Count than that fool Horold. . . .

That same evening a council of war was being held in the ruin-avenue cut by the Count's laser. Just visible through the trees on either side were the clearings of two Warrior Plant-Mothers. Assembled here, seated on fallen tree fragments, were all the leaders of the Wheel, including Will and even Porphyry; also Myrto of Westron, now a Wilding woman, and her young charge the faun-girl Cleito.

"Will," said Cleito, when the men had made a pause in their discussion, "if you are going forward against that laser tomorrow, can't I come too? I—I don't want to live without you."

"But that might be your duty, my dear," said Will soberly, taking her hand and pressing it. "You are going to be Countess of Westron, as Myrto once foretold. Whether I am also to be Count, I think tomorrow will decide."

"Wait!" cried Myrto suddenly, springing up. "You may be Count earlier that that, Prince Elric." She was holding her hands to her head. "Ambrose ..." she murmured, shutting her eyes.

Porphyry also was on his feet. "Yes—yes!" he said. "I perceive it, too. It is starting."

"What is starting?" exclaimed Ferbrand.

"The Turn of the Wheel," said Porphyry. "The hour that has been preparing for years, for centuries. Not yet in Endor, but in Westria. In Westron, now ..."

That same evening in Westron the streets of the capital resounded to the tramp of armed men—men in green tunics and conical helmets. They marched up from the lower docks, through narrow streets where the people cowered in their houses, full of hate and fear. The marines of Akhor—where were they going? To burn down another covenstead, as they had done so often in the past few weeks? But there seemed too many of them for such a small persecution as that. And they were being led by a well-known and well-hated figure—the young Emir Barak himself.

The people in the quarter next to the Agency citadel were the first to guess the truth.

For the past two weeks the Agency buildings had been under cautious siege by the Count Horold's men. The more hot-headed among the Swordist Knights had urged an attack—after all, the gates could hardly withstand a real onslaught. But the Count had been deterred from this move by political considerations. An overt attack on an Agency establishment might well unite all Atlantis against him. As it was, Trinovant was mobilized, and there were now mutterings from Tanis and Suthron, the counties which faced Akhor across the narrowest seas and therefore feared the Count's new allies most.

Barak smiled as the Agency walls came in sight. Well, it would not be the Count now who would be blamed for the attack! This nest of idolatrous Science must be wiped out, to give Akhor a secure foothold in Westria.

At his command the marines moved swiftly into the houses on either side of the street. The Count's holding forces, to their great surprise, found themselves bundled unceremoniously out of their positions.

"By what authority are we relieved?" cried one of the Westrian captains.

"By the authority of this," grinned Barak, holding out his sword.

The Westrians trickled away. Some of them went at once to the upper docks near the Palace, where the Westrian navy ships were moored. Here the Westrian naval captains received them, and listened to their story.

Meanwhile, Barak had launched his assault. The gates did not stand up long. As they crashed in ruin under the battering ram, Barak himself leaped from his cover, and charged in at the head of his men.

A few minutes later, the Akhorians were reeling out of the citadel. Some clutched their heads, some screamed, others laughed hideously, mindlessly. Barak himself wandered, alone and disarmed, into a side street. Here he was set upon and knifed by a certain shopkeeper, a normally peaceable Westrian whose brother had lived, till that spring, in the village of Ringston.

The time was now after sunset, but the midsummer twilight still lingered. Men ran through the streets of Westron, many of them toward the docks. The sailors on guard in the Akhorian flotilla suddenly noticed that the Westrian ships were unmooring.

"Treachery!" shouted Kherev, the Emir's Commodore. "Let us meet these heathen, then! Cast off! Rowers, ready! The Lord will protect his own."

But the threatened naval battle in the Sabrina never took place. As the fleets drifted toward each other in the twilight, the Westrian lookouts saw, to their amazement, that the enemy ships were settling steadily deeper into the water. And without a single missile cast or a blow struck, every Akhorian vessel sank peacefully into the depths of the river.

The survivors, struggling in the water, found that there were other swimmers beside them—creatures that were only vaguely man-shaped, with round heads and webbed fingers.

Kherev was rescued by one of the Westrian ships. All the fight had gone out of him. He told the Westrian captain:

"We kept a good watch at all times. But your secret divers must be artisans of genius."

"What secret divers?" exclaimed the Westrian. "We used none!"

"Then," said Kherev, "how comes it that our ships were scuttled? There were secret holes bored in a hundred places, held plugged till the last moment, and then pulled out!"

As they spoke, a round-headed creature surfaced and blew close beside the ship. In his webbed paw he was holding up a metal knife and a piece of cord.

That same evening, all over those parts of Westria which were still held by Swordist lords in the name of Count Horold, the faun servants were quietly disappearing from the houses of many human masters. In a few cases, where the masters had behaved abominably, the fauns did not leave living masters behind them.

At Alvern, young Hugo Brunner had been amusing himself in his bedchamber whipping a little naked human girl with blue-dyed hair. While still engaged in this sport, he was set upon and strangled by a couple of male fauns, the shepherd Skiptoe and his brother. At almost the same moment, Lucy, Lily and other nymph maids took knives from the kitchen and stabbed to death Baroness Alvern, Norbert's wife. After that they found decent human clothing and put it upon the former slave woman Joan Mack and her little daughter.

Mistress Mack and her child were in tears. But Lucy and Lily kissed them, and did their best to comfort them.

"Fear nothing, Joan," said Lucy seriously. "From now on there will be no more wicked humans in Westria, and neither fauns nor humans will be slaves."

In the Palace of Westron, the Chamberlain Nemon opened the gates of the outer courtyard to the sailors of the Westrian navy.

"Goddess save Count Elric," called Nemon calmly, as the men stormed in. "We are all of your party here, good captains. But you shall not hurt the women—the young Count would not like that."

"Come on, come on, *animal*," cried one of the sailors. "Thirty-six concubines and two wives! Out of our way—"

"Guards!" rapped Nemon.

At once a line of green fauns appeared on the steps of the Great Hall building. Every one was armed with a tubolia pike, metal-tipped; and many of the pike tips were already red. Above, in the hall windows, more fauns appeared, bending arrows to their bows.

"We have already slain every human guard who resisted us," said Nemon, almost apologetically. "Unfortunately, that was necessary. We are well posted here, behind cover, and well armed. I shall continue to hold this Palace in the name of Count Elric until I receive His Highness' personal instructions. Do not attempt to advance any further, or you will be sorry for it."

The sailors drew back, muttering, and then the situation was saved, as green-robed men pushed their way into the Palace yard.

"The Peace of the Covenant be upon you all," said Ambrose. "Sailors, save your blows for your real enemies. If you would not be slaves of Akhor, finish off the traitors who admitted those pirates into your country. Take your ships, and sail upriver; and send a messenger to your good Count Elric. You will find him with his army before Mandrake End."

In the tented camp at Mandrake End, the Count Horold, tossing uneasily on his pallet, called to his Chamberlain Narses. There was no one else in the tent, for the Count did not now tolerate the presence of any man near him while he slept.

"Narses," he said, "what time is it?"

"After midnight, my lord."

Horold considered. "Sword dammit, I can't sleep! Narses, I suppose there's no news—from Westron, or anywhere else?"

"No my lord."

Horold grunted. "Your famous intuition isn't working

so well now, it seems. Not like when you warned me of Barak's raid on Ringston. Can't you use your second sight now?"

"My lord, the power is fitful," said Narses. "It comes and goes. I feel now indeed a sense of great events. By this time tomorrow, this war will be decided."

"Oh, so you're a fortuneteller as well?" said Horold, grinning bitterly. "Well, what sort of fortune do you foresee for us? Good or bad?"

Narses looked at him pensively. "Sire, for yourself I foresee nothing. For myself, likewise. There is a kind of great blank which stops my thought."

Horold grunted. "Cheerful, aren't you? Well, Narses, get out now, and make sure you guard the door of my tent, and see to the other guards round about. I must be fresh for tomorrow."

"My lord," said Narses, looking round at the primitive oil lamp, "shall I put out the light?"

"No, you fool," roared the Count. "I've got to see if I have to shoot."

There was not yet any grayness, and yet the dawn could not be far off. Here and there among the tents burned planted torches, and there were men tending them, and guards making their rounds. There were several guards around the Count's tent, and the ground here was quite brightly lit. The next tents on either side housed the two legitimate Princes, Steelmon and Ferizel. They might quite comfortably have shared a single tent, but they did not trust each other well enough for that. Steelmon, the heir, was the son of the First Countess; Ferizel the son of the Second.

Now among the shadows one of the Count's guards saw two men approaching. He held up his torch. Maybe he ought to challenge, call the other guards—but it was only Lord Basil and Baron Norbert, doubtless bringing important news.

"Why—" he began; and then Norbert's sword leaped.

Basil caught the torch as it fell from the hand of the dead man. Good, he had not had time to cry out!

"Take his pike, Norbert," he whispered. "That's right. Now, follow."

They stalked around the great tent until they reached

the doorway. This was the most critical moment: they would have to silence both Narses and the human guard there at once, without the slightest fumbling.

"You take that damned animal," breathed Basil. "I—"

He stopped. The tent door was unguarded! There was just one figure there, a body sprawled. Immediately he guessed, and leaped through the doorway.

Yes, there at the sleeping Count's head he saw the faun, stealthily stooping, his hand at the pillow. So even this animal had thought—

Basil struck. As the faun toppled, the Count awakened.

"Treachery—" he screamed, scrabbling under his pillow. But Narses' fingers had displaced the gun just enough.

"Here's for you, *brother*," laughed Basil, his rapier finding Horold's heart.

An instant later, Norbert was beside him. "My lord—" he began in his usual smooth manner. But things were altered now.

Basil drew the laser from under the pillow.

"Keep your distance, Baron," he said, "and call me Highness."

It seemed that Horold's last cry had been heard. Soldiers were tumbling out of the tents, and among them came the Princes Steelmon and Ferizel, each with drawn sword, each glaring at the other.

"Traitor!" cried Steelmon, waving his weapon. "My father, the Count—"

"Your father is no longer the Count," said a grim voice.

A man was standing in the doorway of the Sovereign's tent, with a second man, Baron Norbert, standing some meters off on his right. "Kneel, all of you," said Basil.

There was enough torchlight to see that he was holding the laser.

"Basil," cried Ferizel feverishly, "let's talk this over. We can all share—"

Basil's laser swept.

"Now," he said comfortably to the shrinking soldiers, "you will all obey me, men of Westron. I am the only Count or Prince left in this army."

Chapter
FIFTEEN

When two antagonists both know that the advantage lies with the defense, the onset is very likely to be delayed. It was for this reason, perhaps among others, that the Battle of Mandrake End did not begin promptly at sunrise on June 12th, 976.

Basil's Westrian army to start with had the advantage of light behind them. On the other hand, they had the disadvantage of an enigmatic line of black trees before them, and half of them had already had one bad experience with native Dextran trees in their front. In addition, Basil did not very much trust his troops. He decided, therefore, not to attack, but disposed his forces north and south down the slopes of the inverted-bowl-shaped hill, leaving a sizeable gap at the very summit, where Basil stood himself, laser in hand.

Will, crouching behind the line of Mandrakes in the stream bed, spoke to his leading Knights and Handler centaurs.

"The longer we stand here, the more nervous he will become. Actually, he can hardly move at all, either forward or back. We hold nearly all of Westria except for this one hill, even though he does not know it yet. You can do everything with a terror-weapon except sit on it—as he will shortly discover. I would wait days, except that we can't afford *that* much time for other reasons. For instance, Trinovant is moving. Give him till this afternoon."

Helenus the centaur said: "And then, my lord Count, I request the honor of the first charge."

"Granted," said Will, "provided I have the honor of the second, I and my Knights of the Wheel."

By midday the weather was extremely hot, and the Westrian soldiers on their hill were sweating under their jerkins. They would certainly have abandoned the field, and the war, but for the knowledge that they would have been slaughtered at once by Basil's laser.

One hour of the afternoon passed. The second hour passed. The Westrian soldiers were now lying down on the sloping field, and a deputation of knights were expostulating with Basil.

"Back," said Basil, gritting his teeth. "Back, or I fire at once."

A single knight broke ranks and rode his hexip straight at Basil. Basil slaughtered both mount and rider with a single motion of his arm.

"You see," he said. "To your posts at once, gentlemen, or—"

At that moment, the centaurs struck.

The Myrmies came trotting up the hill from the southwest, more or less out of the sun, in an extended line. Basil promptly began cutting them down. But the centauroids came on calmly, not in the least dismayed by their casualties. They had lost all their first wave, and half, two-thirds of their second, and still they came on with unabated ferocity. Now a hundred of them had ridden past Basil's line of fire, and struck the left flank of the Westrian forces with lance, club, hoof or nails. Before this charge the footsoldiers simply melted away, and the Swordist Knights, left unsupported, fared little better. In minutes, the entire left wing of Basil's army had ceased to exist.

Basil grinned, and fanned his laser across the now clear line of fire. All the Myrmies disintegrated—all, that is, except the last one, the Myrmie warrior who was farthest around to the west. This six-limbed monster came on unperturbed, though Basil frantically pressed his laser button again and again.

"Guards!" he screamed at last. "Forward! Cut him down!"

The Westrian Knights nearest to Basil in the right wing of the army thundered across the field: evidently they had not grasped the significance of Basil's plight. Led by Norbert Brunner, dozens of them plowed into the solitary Myrmie, and the centauroid went down fighting.

Then Will rose up from his post among the Mandrake trees, and mounted the Myrmie that had stood by him all the while. All along the line, the other Wheel Knights were doing the same.

"Damn him," growled Ferbrand, "I thought his blasted blaster was going to last forever!"

Will grinned. "Everything ends," he said. "And now, let's make an end of this. Gentlemen, brothers, for the Wheel, and Westria!"

When Basil saw the blue-cloaked Knights riding their monstrous mounts up the hill from the west and north, he threw away his useless, empty laser and mounted a hexip and drew his sword.

"For Westron!" he shouted. "For Westron!" And he dug his spurs into his beast and charged down the slope.

Halfway down the hill he encountered a young brown-eyed Wheel Knight. Basil had raised his sword for a vicious cut at his opponent's head, when the knight's Myrmie mount reached forward and swung his claws at the hexip's eyes. The hexip immediately shied and threw Basil to the ground—in Dextran gravity, and in armor, a terrible fall.

But the Swordist staggered to his feet as Will alighted from his mount, and the two antagonists confronted each other, sword in hand.

"Yield, Basil," said Will. "You are already defeated. The whole of Westria is mine. Look around you: your Knights are being slaughtered, and my sailors are in your rear. You cannot escape."

"So—you are the so-called New Count," said Basil, striking savagely. Will parried, leaping aside.

"No—I am the old one," he said. "I was Count of Westron nearly twenty years ago when your family slaughtered mine. Now yield yourself, Invader."

They were striking blow for blow. Nearby, the Swordist Knights' numbers were dwindling, and their line was already broken into little pockets of mostly dismounted men, and now Handler centaurs were flinging themselves into the fray with savage yells. The battle was clearly decided.

THE WILDINGS OF WESTRON

"Well," panted Basil, "do you offer me life and pardon—a safe conduct?"

"No," said Will coolly. "I offer you merely death without useless struggle. Mercy to you, Basil, would be a mistake. I know you of old. Do you remember Rondel, whom you once tortured? I am he."

"You lie," said Basil wildly, striking again, a whirling blow. "Rondel was flayed."

"I am also Elric, who was also flayed; and Will the Wanderer—flayed again. I am all your victims, Basil. I am your death."

Basil struck once more, desperately. Will did not parry this blow, he jumped clean aside. And as Basil passed him, carried on downhill by how own impetus, he raised his sword and brought it down, once, in a powerful cut.

Basil's head flew from his body, and the headless corpse continued down the slope several paces till it collapsed in a horrible heap; and the Battle of Mandrake End was over.

Will smiled and sheathed his sword. And before him now stood Ferbrand, who tossed another severed head onto the ground at his feet.

"Norbert Brunner, that was," said Ferbrand. "He begged me for mercy, at the end. But I cut him down. We have cut nearly all of them down, Will—hardly one Swordist lord has escaped this field."

"Good," said Will, clapping Ferbrand on the shoulder. "Well done, brother. Of some people, it's best to make a clean sweep."

One war was now over, and it would be pleasant to record that Count Elric William IV of Westron entered his capital city at once in triumph. But history is not always as neat as fiction, and we honest librarians of Evenor, and historians of the great year 976, must merely register the messy truth. On the very field of Mandrake End, that evening, Count Will received the news that the army of Trinovant had crossed the border and was marching on Arlow, the first vital point on the route for Westron.

"The Governor is calling it a cyclade," said the panting messenger.

Will laughed. "A nice expression for a Swordist! If ever there was a cyclade, it is over. What news of Akhor?"

"That is why they are marching, Sire," said the man. "The navies of Tanis and Trinovant joined together, and defeated the Old Emir off the mouth of the Isis—not with great loss, but enough. There is no longer a threat to Atlantis from the pirates, at least not till the Emir can lick his wounds."

"Why then," said Will, "so much the better. Ho for Trinovant!"

And so the new campaign started. It is not necessary for our purposes to record it in detail; but in brief, within two weeks the combined forces of Evenor plus marines from the Westrian navy met the Trinovantians just across the Sabrina from Arlow, at the field of Easter Down; and the army of Count Elric had the victory, and (in the old phrase) held the place of slaughter. In this battle many Swordist lords of the surname Harkness were left on the field, and the remnant of the Trinovantians fled back to their famous capital in great disorder and shame.

"Now," said Will, as he surveyed the piles of corpses, and Ferbrand told him the list of their names, "at last my poor family are in some degree avenged. We shall deal further with Trinovant and the Governor; but now we have earned a breathing space. Gentlemen and brothers, let us turn our Myrmies toward Westron. Or rather, Ferbrand—you shall lead the army there. I must first return to the borders of Evenor."

Almost the first thing that Cleito saw, when she rode into Westron under the West Gate, was the stuffed skin of Rondel, the sixteen-year-old traitor page. The moment might have been tragic, but was not—because Will at that very moment was riding by her side, alive and well.

The body had been left there deliberately: all that had been done to it was that it had been clothed in an imitation of life, with the front parts of the doublet and hose of a young gentle page. And in this guise, the stuffed skin was not even horrible any more.

"O Will," said Cleito, "what a beautiful young boy you were—and yet already a worrior!"

It was only after the triumphal procession had passed

THE WILDINGS OF WESTRON

the gate that the bodies of the "traitors" were to be taken down. A good number of the same traitors were even then riding under that Gate.

"On," said the young Count. "To the Church of the Ring!"

All Westron seemed to be out in holiday attire that Midsummer Eve, and there were as many fauns as humans in the streets, fauns dressed as the whim had taken them, some in sarongs, some in humanlike doublets or tunics, and some in the most authentic and native faun garb of nothing but a few flowers. Among the riders in the procession, besides Porphyry and many Wheel Knights and Ambrose and many Agency scientists, there were also green and gold fauns of Evenor—at the head of whom rode King Silvius and Queen Melisande. By decree of the new Count, not only had slavery of any species been abolished in Westria, but fauns of any color were now endowed with full citizen rights.

Many humans were surprised to find how little practical difference this made in the relations between themselves and their faun servants. The wiser folk guessed that the fauns had never really been property at all, but rather voluntary servants—and spies: spies of the Goddess, or of the planet Dextra as represented by the Mothers.

As the riders moved slowly on past the Gate, the cheers of the bystanders became almost deafening. We think it likely that Cleito drew even more applause than Count Will, for though everyone loved and honored the young Count, the fauns and nymphs had a special bias in favor of that slight green-skinned lass who was both woman and nymph at once.

The cavalcade—or rather Myrmicade—now reached the main square of Westron. Cleito looked up at the massive sandstone arches of the Cathedral front, and remembered that terrible day, less than three months previously, when she had stood here and felt the lustful gaze of Count Horold bent upon her. But those days were over now, both for herself and for Westron, gone like a nightmare from which one had awoken.

And now the Chief Witch, the High Priestess Myrto, stood in white-and-purple robe before the doors of the Cathedral to welcome them.

"Blessed be!" called Myrto.

"Blessed be," replied Will. He alighted from his steed and helped Cleito off her own. Then he turned once more to Myrto, and said:

"High Priestess, here are two faithful followers of the Goddess who wish to be handfasted, truly handfasted in single and perpetual marriage, according to the original and decent customs of Evenor and Westria." And he pointed to himself and Cleito.

A great cheer went up from the fauns in the square. From the humans, the noise was more confused: some cheers, but also many gasps.

Myrto looked solemn. "There is no custom," she said, "of marriage between folk of different *species*. And certainly no marriage of a green faun."

"Why," said Will, smiling, "if I may quote from one of the old books of Tellus, that I have read in the Glass Castle, nice customs curtsy to great kings. And if I am not quite a great king yet, Myrto, I assure you I mean to be—King of Atlantis, no less—at least, for a time."

"But marriage implies issue," said Myrto, suppressing a smile. "Offspring."

"Come, my dear Witch," said Will, "has no one told you our little secret yet? But I do not wish to make my sweet bride blush!"

At this there was a great roar of laughter and cheers from the crowd; and Myrto gracefully capitulated. The wedding of Will and Cleito, of young man and young nymph, was celebrated at once, in the circular nave of the great Cathedral.

Afterward, as Cleito kissed Will, she murmured:

"Thank you, darling, for making an honest nymph of me!"

"And now," said Will, "we will proceed to the Palace for the marriage feast."

At the Palace, the first person to welcome them was Nemon, whom Will had confirmed in office as First Chamberlain of Westria. Nemon smiled, but Cleito was nymph enough to feel his melancholy; he had not yet recovered from the death of his twin brother Narses.

"Nemon," said Cleito, remembering, "I have also lost— one gentle friend."

"Thank you," said Nemon quietly. "Your Highnesses, is there aught you would wish to see in the Palace before the feast?"

Cleito looked at Will; Will nodded.

"Yes: the Tower of the Women!"

Nemon led them up to the dilapidated courtyard. These traitors too had been clothed. Cleito had been expecting the shock—but still it was a shock, and a much worse one than Westgate. For there they stood, pinned up on the wall—herself and Will, in their own human shapes, just as they had been but two months earlier. The fair-skinned blue-eyed womanly Cleito stared glassily down at the green-skinned little nymph.

Cleito burst into tears.

"My darling," said Will, holding her, "we will have them all burned, immediately."

"No," said Cleito, drying her eyes. "No, let them be kept somewhere, my Prince. After all, they are not terrible—not one of them died! Every one is just a stage—and all life passes through stages; nothing really dies. That is the meaning of the Ring, of the Wheel, isn't it?"

"Yes," said Will, his manly fingers brushing Cleito's pointed ears and blue hair. "That's some of it. I shall be glad when this stage of yours is over, my dear."

"Six months," said Cleito, gritting her teeth, "six more months."

The feast in the Great Hall that night was a most joyful one. All the notables of Evenor were present, and a great many dignitaries of Westria. (There were present even a couple of librarians from the Glass Castle, so we can guarantee this account as highly authentic.) Among so many friends, it is hard to single out individuals. Most touching, perhaps, was the presence at the high table of old Sir Richard Lee and his wife Bessy, and of Joan Mack and her two young children.

As royal protocol demanded, in the places of honor were seated King Silvius and Queen Melisande—but Cleito still called her friend Melissa, even as she called her husband Will, and her gold-skinned friend did not resent this.

"Nay, Cleity," she said, laughing, "what have I to be proud *about*? I am now only what the Mother made me, through the favor of my dear husband. Let us not put on airs, for Goddess' sake!"

"Quite right, Melly," said Will, leaning over and whispering. "I am going to be King for a while—Porphyry and Ambrose demand it of me—but one day soon, I hope, Kings will be no more needed in Atlantis, no, nor Counts neither. Till then—why, it's just another stage, another skin to wear and then cast!"

There were quite a few unattached ladies at the feast. The former Countesses had been allowed to depart to their Harkness relatives in Trinovant, but at least half of the thirty-six concubines of Count Horold had elected to stay in Westron, and were found places in the body of the hall that night. Cleito noticed with amusement that several seemed to be ogling the younger and more handsome Knights of the Wheel. But there was one ex-concubine who was seated at the high table: Estrild of Nordica. She had a seat next to the Count's foster brother Ferbrand, and she certainly did not need to ogle him.

"Another bad case!" said Cleito, laughing quietly and nudging Will. Ferbrand's green eyes were fixed on Estrild's blue ones; he seemed quite fascinated. "Well, why not? Estrild's a good girl at heart—I'll never forget how she befriended me, the only one of that lot. She should make Ferbrand at least as good a wife as, say, Jacynth."

They looked at the pair down the table: now Estrild was laughing, touching glasses with Ferbrand, her blue eyes sparkling.

"I think he's making it," said Will smiling. "Good old Ferbrand! He was always a success with the girls at the Glass Castle, but he never took any of them too seriously. This looks different, now."

One small problem at this feast was the two very different types of food and drink served. For once in this hall, at least half the guests as well as the sovereign pair were dining off native food—parabread and kin-nuts and Golden Apples. And already, fashion being what it is, many dignitaries of Westron were enquiring the way to the Great Mothers in Evenor.

Ferbrand called across to Will: "The Lady Estrild wants to be translated to Wilding flesh. May I take her there tomorrow, brother?"

"I believe you can take her whenever you like," said Will, straight-faced. "But yes, get her changed; it will be nicer for you both that way."

At Will's request, Porphyry made a speech to the assembled guests.

"There has been much dissension in the past," he said, "between the sects of the Ring and of the Sword. Some counties of Atlantis favor one, some the other. This was always an unnecessary quarrel. May it be past and done with now forever. From henceforth, I am authorized by your gracious Count to announce, the badge of this County will be the Wheel—which combines in one device the Sword, crosswise in the center, and the Ring. The Sword must be in the Ring, if union is to be fertile."

"As all true children of the Goddess know," added Myrto, smiling sweetly, "and as this Midsummer Night's liturgy makes clear."

After they had drunk the customary toasts, Will led Cleito away to a great bedchamber—not the one used by the tyrant Horold, but another which held no terrible memories.

"My love, my love," said Will, when they were both naked, holding Cleito's little green body to him. It was the first time they had lain together since Will had become a man once more. The room was dimly lit by a single shaded lamp, and through the window by the gleams of some three Dextran moons.

"O my dear," said Cleito, almost shyly, touching his face with the four slim fingers of her right hand, "I love being married to you, but I wish I could give you pleasure."

"Do you really imagine you can't?" said Will, laughing shortly, "You're wrong, my little Chloe. I still want you, immensely, and in that shape you're utterly charming. But you—men can't pleasure nymphs."

"No?" said Cleito. "I wonder. Will, this is Midsummer Night. With the help of the Ring Goddess and the Sword God, you know strange witchcrafts can be accomplished."

"And where there's a Will, there's a way," laughed Will. "Yes, my darling: yes . . ."

Well, as Cleito told it to us afterward—she had no false modesty, our gracious young Countess—they managed;

not as perfectly perhaps as when they were both fauns, but enough for true delight. A man's tongue cannot reach a nymph's pleasure buds, but if she helps him properly, his fingers can. And those two were both of kin flesh, and could feel each other's joy, and the Sword was not only in the Ring, it helped to establish something like that other ring which is the bliss and glory of nymphs and fauns. . . .

Six months can sometimes seem an eternity. It is not so for an active young war leader who is winning victories and molding the destinies of nations, but it is a great while for a pregnant lady, whether human or nymph, who perforce must sit at home and wait anxiously for news of her husband from foreign Counties or across the seas. So it proved for Cleito through the summer and autumn of 976. Mostly she lived in the Palace of Westron, experiencing in her inmost being the progress of her unhuman pregnancy, and waiting for the next messenger from the Agency with the latest radio report of Will's dangers and battles.

To her great joy, no harm came to Will, not even a wound in any of his campaigns, but success after success. First he led the forces of Evenor and Westria against Trinovant, and in one decisive battle utterly crushed the House of Harkness, the Governor Havion himself being found dead among the fallen. The great capital on the Isis made no resistance, but peaceably invited Will to enter the First City of Atlantis and assume the title of Governor, which he did. But Trinovant was no resting place for the forces of the Wheel. Immediately, the Emir Melek was reported at sea with his whole fleet.

This was precisely the opportunity which Will had most desired. His envoys went to every County of Atlantis, and nearly every County responded favorably. Certainly, Tanis, Suthron, Amaurot and Camlan sent ships and men, and very soon Will found himself admiral of a great combined fleet. Together, the Wheel Knights and the men of the Counties defeated the old Emir—not only at sea but also on his own ground, for they invaded Akhor and forced the Saintly pirates to submit to a crippling peace. One clause of this peace was that slavery and ownership of fauns were abolished in Akhor, and all captives were freed and allowed to go home.

THE WILDINGS OF WESTRON

One captive, though, preferred not to. Will's knights had just taken a certain pirate stronghold, the former home of the Emir Barak, and the inhabitants were being paraded before the conquerors to check that no slaves were being concealed. Ferbrand was especially thorough in this work, and the beaten pirates groaned with impotent fury as he made the women strip off their long veils and declare their names and origins. Will thought the Akhorian women sometimes pretty, and they were much bedizened in dural bracelets and even little chains about their ankles, but they lacked the spirit of Atlantian girls.

Then, as Ferbrand made one golden-skinned wench unveil, Will started.

"I know that face!" he exclaimed. "It's—isn't it—Alis Carver?"

It was. Alis' hair was rather short, and she wore a steel ankle chain and heavy earrings and long linen robes, but she was quite recognizable. She looked rather indignant.

"Your slavery is over, Alis—" began Will kindly.

"I'm not a slave!" exclaimed Alis, stamping her honey-colored bare foot. "I am fourth wife of the Emir Zahav, I'll have you know, poor Barak's brother, and I protest at this indignity. I'm a decent, respectable Lordist wife—don't you dare to carry me off, you—you—"

"Oh, all right," said Will grimly. "Let her pass, Ferbrand. Poor Cleito! She was unlucky in her relations."

After Akhor, Will went briefly back to Trinovant; and there, in that city of temples and canals, Porphyry crowned him High King of Atlantis, and the various Counts acknowledged his suzerainty. They had little alternative; by now their own warriors, indeed all their peoples, were full of enthusiasm for the brilliant young war leader and his invincible Knights, and there was a constant stream of pilgrims from all over the island, who made their way to the Mothers in Evenor and returned to their homes as men and women of Wilding flesh.

And by now the year was old, and the month was December.

"Just in time, I think," cried Will, soon after his return to the Palace of Westron, when at last he had got Cleito alone in their splendid bedchamber. "Really, I finished those wars just in time, darling."

"Oh," said Cleito, surprised and pleased, "so you can tell, can you?"

"Why, yes," said Will. "I got the message from Ambrose as I rode through Westgate. Things are stirring on the Continent—"

Cleito burst out laughing. "O Will, Will! That's not what I meant. Things are stirring in *me*. And Ambrose couldn't have told you at Westgate, because it's only just begun. Right now!"

"O My Goddess," said Will breathlessly. "Darling, I'll get help—"

"No help needed, Will," said Cleito. "I'm a nymph, remember? Just take off my clothes. And then watch. It should be interesting."

It was.

Actually, even though Cleito had not summoned helpers—not consciously, anyway—the birth of her twins was not a completely private event. Melissa, herself now big with twins, happened to drift in, and after her, half a dozen faun-maids of the Palace.

There were of course no complications of any kind. The marvel accomplished itself in a few seconds, easily, painlessly, as it always does for faun mothers. Faun babies do not even have to cry.

Melissa laughed. "Who'd have thought it," she said, "who would *ever* have thought it, Cleity, that you would have borne little nymphs, and before me, too? Aren't they darlings! Now this is what you must do, to suckle them with your mouth . . ."

Cleito found that that was not difficult either, her mouth, in her present shape, was designed for it. But after a while she inquired about the availability of nymph wet-nurses; and was glad to hear that there was no problem about this.

"Why then," she said, her eyes gleaming, "Will, there's no reason why we shouldn't set out for Evenor at once. . . ."

And so, on the first day of the New Year, Will and Cleito stood once more before the Great Mothers in that warm forest, with many of their friends around them. At dawn the nymph Cleito entered the huge petal of the

Plant, and at noon the petal burst—and disclosed a human girl, beautiful, black-haired, blue-eyed, with a fair skin; and not yet seventeen years old as years are reckoned on Dextra.

"Cleito, my darling, my Queen," said Will, kissing her lips and seizing her hand. "At last, at last! Queen Cleito of Atlantis!"

"O no, Will," said Cleito. She was naked, but she did not mind this in the least as Will helped her out of the Plant and we all cheered. "Plain Cleito Dixon will do, if Will Turner will do also."

"Will Turner certainly will," said Will, his eyes gleaming.

That is very nearly the end of our story. There remains to add one more circumstance, which will perhaps have more significance for our human readers than for ourselves.

All the evening of New Year's Day was given up to revelry in the Glass Castle. The Lady Bessy of course was there, and took the tiny twin green princesses on her lap; indeed, everyone made a fuss of them, but especially Melissa. We heard her say once to Cleito:

"You know, Cleity, while you were inside the petal I spoke to the Mothers. They told me I am going to have boy twins. When they are all the right age, I think we should encourage our pairs to be mates."

"What, humans and goldskins?" laughed Cleito. "Your boys will be too proud to have them, I think."

"Why should your girls become *humans?*" said Melissa. "Their true nature is this—what they are now, nymphs. Let them remain so! You know, they would probably be *very naughty* girls.... And you will have other, *truly* human children by Will. If you want to have these little ones changed, why not change them just a little—into goldies like us?"

"We are indeed the true perfection of faundom," said King Silvius, nodding in stately agreement.

Cleito looked at Will. He smiled.

"Let us have our little ones to make up their own minds," he said. "But I would be proud to have two gold-skinned Goddesses for daughters."

"Oh, Will, it's wonderful!" said Cleito.

She was looking at her hands, moving her extra, fifth finger, and feeling her own skin, radiating joy in simply being *herself* completely—we might have said "again," but "again" is not quite the right word. This was Cleito's first day of life in her final instar, as a Wilding human girl. She tried to express her feelings, and it did not matter when words failed her, for being kin-flesh she was communicating with Will and all her friends all the time. She was even communicating with a pair of humble Gobblers, who are now recording this scene.

"O, this is the best of all!" she said at last. "Will and I—we are really human together at last. The mingling of minds—and no darkness left in the flesh."

"Talking of flesh," said Will, standing up, "my dear, you know we have not yet consummated our marriage as *human* beings. Why, you are practically a virgin!"

Everyone laughed as those two swept out of the hall, on their way to great happiness. But the joke was on us—

—For next morning, in our library, we received a breathless visit from Queen Melisande/Melissa.

"Put this down in your chronicle," she said, giggling. "You know, human girls have this funny little piece of flesh, before they have been mated. 'Tis called a maidenhead."

"We have heard of it," we said, waving at the copious stacks of Tellurian literature on our shelves.

"Well—would you believe it! Cleity never *had* really lost hers when she was in human shape, before. So the Mother, when she restored Cleity's human shape yesterday—she restored that too! Cleity had her babies—but she had her maidenhead as well!"

"No!" we said, incredulous.

"Yes," said Queen Melissa. "But she really has lost it now, at last."

HERE ENDS THE CHRONICLE OF

THE WILDINGS OF WESTRON

COMPILED FROM AUTHENTIC SOURCES

BY

THE LIBRARIANS OF SIDERION IN EVENOR

D.E. 977

DAW BOOKS

Lin Carter's bestselling series

- [ ] **UNDER THE GREEN STAR.** A marvel adventure in the grand tradition of Burroughs and Merritt. Book I.
(#UY1185—$1.25)

- [ ] **WHEN THE GREEN STAR CALLS.** Beyond Mars shines the beacon of exotic adventure. Book II. (#UY1267—$1.25)

- [ ] **BY THE LIGHT OF THE GREEN STAR.** Lost amid the giant trees, nothing daunted his search for his princess and her crown. Book III. (#UY1268—$1.25)

- [ ] **AS THE GREEN STAR RISES.** Adrift on the uncharted sea of a nameless world, hope still burned bright. Book IV.
(#UY1156—$1.25)

- [ ] **IN THE GREEN STAR'S GLOW.** The grand climax of an adventure amid monsters and marvels of a far-off world. Book V. (#UY1216—$1.25)

DAW BOOKS are represented by the publishers of Signet and Mentor Books, THE NEW AMERICAN LIBRARY, INC.

THE NEW AMERICAN LIBRARY, INC.,
P.O. Box 999, Bergenfield, New Jersey 07621

Please send me the DAW BOOKS I have checked above. I am enclosing
$_____(check or money order—no currency or C.O.D.'s).
Please include the list price plus 35¢ a copy to cover mailing costs.

Name_____

Address_____

City_____ State_____ Zip Code_____

Please allow at least 4 weeks for delivery

DAW BOOKS sf

Presenting JOHN NORMAN in DAW editions...

☐ **SLAVE GIRL OF GOR.** The eleventh novel of Earth's orbital counterpart makes an Earth girl a puppet of vast conflicting forces. The 1977 Gor novel. (#UJ1285—$1.95)

☐ **TRIBESMEN OF GOR.** The tenth novel of Tarl Cabot takes him face to face with the Others' most dangerous plot—in the vast Tahari desert with its warring tribes. (#UE1296—$1.75)

☐ **HUNTERS OF GOR.** The saga of Tarl Cabot on Earth's orbital counterpart reaches a climax as Tarl seeks his lost Talena among the outlaws and panther women of the wilderness. (#UE1294—$1.75)

☐ **MARAUDERS OF GOR.** The ninth novel of Tarl Cabot's adventures takes him to the northland of transplanted Vikings and into direct confrontation with the enemies of two worlds. (#UE1295—$1.75)

☐ **TIME SLAVE.** The creator of Gor brings back the days of the caveman in a vivid lusty new novel of time travel and human destiny. (#UW1204—$1.50)

☐ **IMAGINATIVE SEX.** A study of the sexuality of male and female which leads to a new revelation of sensual liberation. (#UJ1146—$1.95)

DAW BOOKS are represented by the publishers of Signet and Mentor Books, THE NEW AMERICAN LIBRARY, INC.

THE NEW AMERICAN LIBRARY, INC.,
P.O. Box 999, Bergenfield, New Jersey 07621

Please send me the DAW BOOKS I have checked above. I am enclosing
$_____(check or money order—no currency or C.O.D.'s).
Please include the list price plus 35¢ a copy to cover mailing costs.

Name_____

Address_____

City_____ State_____ Zip Code_____

Please allow at least 4 weeks for delivery

DAW BOOKS sf

- [ ] **WALKERS ON THE SKY** by David J. Lake. Three worlds in one was the system there—until the breakthrough!
(#UY1273—$1.25)

- [ ] **THE RIGHT HAND OF DEXTRA** by David J. Lake. It's the green of Terra versus the purple of that alien world—with no holds barred. (#UW1290—$1.50)

- [ ] **THE GAMEPLAYERS OF ZAN** by M. A. Foster. It's a game of life and death for both humans and their own creation—the not-quite-super race. (#UJ1287—$1.95)

- [ ] **NAKED TO THE STARS** by Gordon R. Dickson. A classic of interstellar warfare as only the Dorsai author could write! (#UW1278—$1.50)

- [ ] **EARTHCHILD** by Doris Piserchia. Was this the only true human left on Earth . . . and who were the monsters that contended for this prize? (#UW1308—$1.50)

- [ ] **DIADEM FROM THE STARS** by Jo Clayton. She became the possessor of a cosmic treasure that enslaved her mind. (#UW1293—$1.50)

DAW BOOKS are represented by the publishers of Signet and Mentor Books, THE NEW AMERICAN LIBRARY, INC.

THE NEW AMERICAN LIBRARY, INC.,
P.O. Box 999, Bergenfield, New Jersey 07621

Please send me the DAW BOOKS I have checked above. I am enclosing $_____(check or money order—no currency or C.O.D.'s). Please include the list price plus 35¢ a copy to cover mailing costs.

Name_____

Address_____

City_____State_____Zip Code_____

Please allow at least 4 weeks for delivery